HARLEQUIN® Presents

Happy New Year! Have you made any resolutions for 2007?

The editors of Harlequin Presents books have made their resolution: to continue doing their very best to bring you the ultimate in emotional excitement every month during the coming year—stories that totally deliver on compelling characters, dramatic story lines, fabulous foreign settings, intense feelings and sizzling sensuality!

January gets us off to a good start with the best selection of international heroes—two Italian playboys, two gorgeous Greek tycoons, a French count, a debonair Brit, a passionate Spaniard and a handsome Aussie. Yummy!

We also have the crème de la crème of authors from around the world: Michelle Reid, Trish Morey, Sarah Morgan, Melanie Milburne, Sara Craven, Margaret Mayo, Helen Brooks and Annie West, who debuts with her very first novel, *A Mistress for the Taking*.

Join us again next month for more of your favorites, including Penny Jordan, Lucy Monroe and Carole Mortimer—seduction and passion are guaranteed!

Harlequin Presents®

GREEK TYCOONS

They're the men who have everything—
except brides...

Wealth, power, charm—
what else could a heart-stoppingly handsome
tycoon need? In the GREEK TYCOONS
miniseries you have already been introduced to
some gorgeous Greek multimillionaires who are
in need of wives.

Now it's the turn of popular Harlequin Presents
author Trish Morey, with her sexy new romance,

The Greek's Virgin

This tycoon has met his match, and he's decided
he *has* to have her...*whatever* that takes!

Coming next month:

The Santorini Bride
by Anne McAllister
#2610

Trish Morey

THE GREEK'S VIRGIN

GREEK
TYCOONS

TORONTO • NEW YORK • LONDON
AMSTERDAM • PARIS • SYDNEY • HAMBURG
STOCKHOLM • ATHENS • TOKYO • MILAN • MADRID
PRAGUE • WARSAW • BUDAPEST • AUCKLAND

ISBN-13: 978-0-373-12596-8
ISBN-10:   0-373-12596-8

THE GREEK'S VIRGIN

First North American Publication 2007.

Copyright © 2006 by Trish Morey.

www.eHarlequin.com

Printed in U.S.A.

All about the author...
Trish Morey

TRISH MOREY wrote her first book at age eleven for a children's book-week competition; entitled *Island Dreamer,* it proved to be her first rejection. Shattered and broken, she turned to a life where she could combine her love of fiction with her need for creativity—and became a chartered accountant. Life wasn't all dull though, as she embarked on a skydiving course, completing three jumps before deciding that she'd given her fear of heights a run for its money.

Meanwhile, she fell in love and married a handsome guy who cut computer code. After the birth of their second daughter, Trish spied an article saying that Harlequin was actively seeking new authors. It was one of those eureka moments—Trish was going to be one of those authors!

Eleven years after reading that fateful article, the magical phone call came and Trish finally realized her dream. According to Trish, writing and selling a book is a major life achievement that ranks right up there with jumping out of an airplane and motherhood. All three take commitment, determination and sheer guts, but the effort is so very, very worthwhile.

Trish now lives with her husband and four young daughters in a special part of south Australia, surrounded by orchards and bushland and visited by the occasional koala and kangaroo.

You can visit Trish at her Web site at www.trishmorey.com or e-mail her at trish@trishmorey.com.

One of the best things about being part of the romance writing community is that you make such fantastic friends, and friends you can call on in a crisis anywhere around the world for brainstorming, plot-storming or just general laughs, inspiration and support. Here's special thanks to just a few of my favorite romance writing friends, many published, some yet to be (but who sure as eggs will be one day!) who never fail to help a fellow writer out in a crisis—

The Wipits—Yvonne Lindsay and Bronwyn Jameson

The Pyrate and Ferret Galz—Anne Gracie, Kelly Hunter and Holly Cook

SA Galz—Kathy Smart, Anne Oliver, Sharon Francesca and Linda Brown

And the entire Wet Noodle Posse (http://www.wetnoodleposse.com)

Without you all, this book would have been written eventually, but it wouldn't have been half as much fun.

Thanks, everyone!

PROLOGUE

Sydney, Australia

BLISS! Life could never get better than this.

Saskia Prentice allowed him to ease her naked body down amongst the soft pillows, her young heart swelling, her lips still humming and swollen from his latest kiss, every cell in her body tingling, plumped and primed in anticipation.

Moonlight stroked against the window, rippling through the silk curtains, turning his skin to satin and illuminating the room in a warm, lunar glow, as if even the heavens approved. And offering just enough light to look up into the dark depths of his eyes as he positioned himself over her. She melted, her body softening even more, as she looked into them.

The eyes of the man she loved.

A moment of crystal-clear clarity pierced the pleasure fog surrounding her as his legs nestled into a welcome place between her own. Not quite eighteen, and already she'd found her soul mate, the one special man on this earth truly destined for her. There was no mistake. He was the one. And they would have years of loving together, years of feeling just like this.

How lucky could one woman get?

Then she stopped thinking and gave herself totally to the

feeling of him pressing against her, wanting to feel him make her his own, wanting to welcome him inside her, compelling him to press harder to unite them and to end this desperate, urgent need…

Their eyes connected briefly as her body began to accept his, as their burning bodies began to meld.

'I love you,' she whispered, putting in words what her heart already knew, her eyelids fluttering closed as she arched against him, urging him to break through that final stinging barrier, urging him to completion.

A second later the bed bucked and all pressure was gone. *He* was gone.

And cold air swept cruelly over the places he'd been.

She opened her eyes, blinking in shock, searching for him. But already he was across the room and dragging on his jeans, throwing on a shirt. And his face was as bleak as the stormiest night, his eyes filled with the darkest savagery.

'Put something on. I'll order you a taxi.'

His voice was coarse and gravelly, and nothing like she'd ever heard before. She looked up at him in horror, feeling suddenly exposed and vulnerable and inadequate all at the same time.

'Alex? What's wrong?'

'*Tsou,*' he spat roughly, tossing his head back as if he was disgusted with himself. His eyes glinted in the moonlight, hard and cold as granite, as he threw her clothes at her on the bed. 'This was a mistake.'

She curled herself behind them as best she could, shame and humiliation flaming her exposed flesh. Was her innocence so much of a turn-off?

'Did I do something wrong? I'm sorry—'

'Get dressed!' he ordered, his words uncompromising, his voice unrecognisable. *The voice of a stranger.*

'But…' Tears pricked at her eyes as she forced back the lump in her throat and fought her way into her clothes. 'But why?'

In the half-light his face was all dark shadows and tight ridges, his muscled body moving with a tenseness tainted with something that simmered like hatred.

'Just get out!' he roared. 'I don't do virgins!'

CHAPTER ONE

London—Eight years later

Success! Saskia Prentice breathed in that sweet smell as she approached the boardroom doors, the high of achievement fizzing in her veins.

In less than five minutes it would be official—she'd become editor-in-chief of the business magazine *AlphaBiz*.

And she'd worked so hard for this!

Twelve months of intense and sometimes bitterly fought competition with fellow journalist Carmen Rivers was proof of that. Carmen had made no secret of the fact that she'd do *anything* to ensure she got the job—and, given her rival's reputation, she probably had. But still it had been Saskia who'd consistently filed the best stories from around the globe, producing the most difficult-to-extract business profiles. Just two days ago the chairman had intimated that she'd won, that the job would be hers come today's board meeting.

She'd been waiting on tenterhooks all day, until at last the summons had come. Finally the job would be hers. And finally she'd have the means to rescue her father from his grungy retirement bedsit and get him a place in a decent care facility in the country. She had it all planned—a small cottage for herself close by with a back garden for him to potter around in on the weekends. The generous sign-on bonus, together with the substantially larger pay packet that went with the job, would make all that possible and more.

One hand on the door latch, the other checking her crazy curls were well slicked down and locked into the tight bun at the nape of her neck, she took one last glorious breath, stringing out the extra buzz of adrenaline at the imminent realisation of her dreams. This was her big chance to make the Prentice name really worth something in business circles once again. And this was her opportunity to give her father back something of the pride that had been so ruthlessly stolen from him.

She let go her breath, tapped lightly on the rich timber doors and let herself in.

Muted sunlight streamed in through the large window, momentarily blinding her. She blinked, surprised, as her eyes adjusted to see not the entire board, as she'd been expecting, but just the chairman, sitting near the head of the table, the sunlight framing his silhouette, transforming him to just a blur of dark against the bright light, his expression indiscernible. In spite of the temperature-controlled air, she shivered.

'Ah, Miss Prentice…*Saskia*,' his voice a low rumble, as he gestured her to sit opposite. 'Thank you so much for coming.'

She responded automatically as she blinked into the light, a disturbing feeling of unease creeping along her spine.

Something was wrong.

Sir Rodney Krieg was a bear of a man, with a booming voice, and yet today he sounded almost gentle. Sir Rodney *never* sounded gentle. And where was the board? Why weren't they all present for the announcement?

The chairman huffed out a long sigh that almost sounded defeated. 'You know that when we organised this meeting we were expecting to be able to formalise our plans to appoint you as the new editor-in-chief?'

She nodded, a sudden tightness in her throat rendering her speechless, feeling his words tugging at the threads of her earlier euphoria.

'Well, I'm afraid there's been a slight change of plans.'

'I don't understand.' She squeezed the words out, battling the crushing chill of disappointment suddenly clamping around her heart, yet still refusing to give up on her dreams just yet. Maybe it was just a delay?

Unless they'd given the job to Carmen after all...

'Has the board decided to go with Carmen instead?'

He shook his head, and for one tiny moment she felt relief.

'Or at least,' Sir Rodney continued, 'not yet.'

And her hopes died anew.

But she wasn't about to go down without a fight. She wouldn't give up on everything she'd worked for that easily. Dry-mouthed, she forced herself to respond, anger building inside. 'What do you mean, "not yet"? What happened? Only two days ago you said—'

He held up one hand to silence her. 'It's irregular, I admit, but Carmen has been having a word in the ear of some of the board members, doing some lobbying on her own behalf...'

Saskia froze. So Carmen had got wind of the board's decision and decided to head it off at the pass? It might be an uncharitable thought, but if Carmen was desperate enough for this position, she didn't want to think about the type of *word* she'd been having in the board members' ears.

'...and to cut a long story short,' Sir Rodney continued, 'the board has decided that a decision as to who is going to head the editorial team shouldn't be rushed.'

'It was hardly rushed,' she protested. 'The board has been deliberating on this for the last twelve months.'

'Nevertheless, the board feels that perhaps Carmen has a point. You've been engaged on different projects during that time. Maybe she hasn't had the opportunity to show her full potential after all.'

Saskia might almost have sneered if she hadn't been more concerned at the mental image of her small cottage in the country misting, the fabric of her dreams unravelling faster than she could tie off the ends. What would she tell her father? With only one, maybe two years of time before his increasing frailty rendered him bedridden, he'd been so looking forward to the move out of the city. She couldn't afford any delays to her plans, let alone risk losing this chance altogether.

'So what happens now?' she asked, her spirits at an all-time low. She'd worked so hard for this opportunity and it had just about been in her grasp. To have it pulled from her reach now, when it had been so close, was more than unfair. 'How long will the board take to make a final decision?'

'Ah. That all depends on you—and Carmen, of course.'

She raised an eyebrow. 'What do you mean?'

Sir Rodney actually managed to look enthusiastic. 'You see, the board has decided that the best way to compare your talents is with a head-to-head contest. You'll each be given a subject we've chosen—in this case, extremely successful businessmen who've chosen to live for whatever reason almost completely out of the public eye. Their public appearances are so rare we know hardly anything about the men themselves, while we see their businesses grow in stature every day. So we want you and Carmen to bring in the goods—what makes them tick? What drives them? The one who brings in the best profile within the month gets their story on the cover of our annual special edition, along with the news of their promotion.'

'But Sir Rodney, I've been consistently turning in great profiles all year—'

'Then one more shouldn't present any problem! I'm sorry, Saskia, but this has come from the board. They want you two to slug it out for the position, and that's what you're going to have to do to get it.'

'I see,' she snipped, hoping her subject wasn't too far flung. With this promotion she'd been counting on an end to her incessant traveling, so she could keep an eye on her father's condition. But she took heart from the time frame. This job couldn't take longer than a month. She'd make sure she did it in less. And then the promotion would be hers. Because she *would* deliver the best profile. There was no question of that! This was no more than a short delay to her plans.

'So who have I been assigned?'

Sir Rodney pushed his glasses on as he lifted up a manila folder lying nearby and flicked open the cover, scanning the information contained within.

'One very interesting character, it appears. You've scored a fellow Sydney-sider who now has extensive interests all over the world. Another one of Australia's Greek success stories, apparently.'

Cold needles of dread crawled up her spine. A Greek Australian from Sydney?

Oh, no way. It couldn't be…

There had to be dozens that fitted that description…

There wasn't a chance in the world…

'A fellow by the name of Alexander Koutoufides. Have you heard of him?'

Every organ and muscle inside Saskia seemed to clamp

down tight, squeezing the air from her lungs and the very blood from her veins. *Had she heard of him?* Part of her wanted to laugh hysterically even as the vacuum in her stomach began to fill with the bitter juices of the past.

He was the man she'd so stupidly imagined herself in love with, the same man who had so savagely thrust her from his bed—right before he'd turned around and coldly destroyed her father's business!

Oh, yes—she'd heard of Alexander Koutoufides!

And there was no way in the world that she was going to profile him. Hell, there was no way she was ever meeting that man again, let alone hanging around long enough to play twenty questions.

Sir Rodney hadn't waited for her response, clearly expecting her to answer in the positive. She forced herself to put aside her shock and focus on his words.

'…seems he made a big splash in business circles until about eight years ago, when he suddenly dropped right out of business circles and became almost a recluse, nonetheless quietly expanding his business interests into the northern hemisphere while refusing all requests for interviews…'

She raised one hand, beseeching him to stop. She didn't need to hear any more. 'I'm sorry, Sir Rodney. I really don't think me doing a profile on Alexander Koutoufides is a very good idea.'

He paused, leaning forward in his chair so slowly that it creaked. 'I'm not actually *asking* whether you think this is a good idea. I'm giving you your assignment!'

'No,' she said. 'Not Alex Koutoufides. It's not going to happen.'

He surveyed her, disbelief unbridled in his eyes, before he slapped the folder back down onto the table. 'But, Saskia, why

on earth would you dip out of this opportunity when the promotion is at stake?'

'Because I've met Alexander Koutoufides. We…' She
licked her lips while she searched for the right words. 'You
might say we have history.'

His eyes widened, glinting with delight as he straightened
in his chair. 'Excellent!' he announced, his voice back to
booming proportions. 'Why didn't you tell me? That should
give you a real head start. I hear our Mr Koutoufides is very
wary of the press—although, given his celebrity sister and her
latest escapades with a certain twenty-something Formula
One driver, that's hardly surprising.'

Saskia blinked as the meaning behind his words registered. 'Marla Quartermain is Alex Koutoufides's sister?' She'd
seen the articles—they'd been impossible to miss after
AlphaBiz's sister magazine, *Snap!*, had run a cover spread on
the scandal that had blown the affair both sky-high and world-
wide. She vaguely remembered he had an older sister, but
they'd never met, and not once had she connected the glam-
orous jet-setter with Alex. 'He sure kept that under wraps.'

'Exactly the way he wanted it, no doubt. It helped that she
took her first husband's name—some joker she married aged
sixteen, only to divorce him less than a year later. The first of
a long string of failed marriages and sad affairs.' He sighed
as he rolled his fountain pen between his fingers. 'But this
time she's obviously gone too far—Alex must have decided
it was time to take control. He was spotted by one of our photographers whisking her out the back entrance of a Sydney
hotel. At first he was assumed to be some new love interest,
but a little digging turned up the family connection—something infinitely more interesting to all concerned.'

Saskia's mind digested the new information. *AlphaBiz's*

sister magazine had been none too complimentary about the aging party girl, charging her with all manner of celebrity crime. Any brother would want to protect his sister from that kind of exposure.

'Given what *Snap!* published about Marla,' she reasoned, putting voice to her concerns, 'Alex is hardly going to be receptive to a request for a profile from this organisation—even if the two magazines are poles apart.'

Sir Rodney held out his hands in a wide shrug. 'That's where your previous relationship will give you the inside running, wouldn't you say?'

'Not a chance,' she stated, shaking her head defiantly. 'Alex Koutoufides…' She paused, choosing her words carefully—Sir Rodney didn't need to know the whole sordid story. 'Well, more than twenty years ago our fathers were in business together in Sydney, but my father struck a deal that saw him whisk Alex's father's business out from under his feet. Alex never forgave him. Eight years ago Alex destroyed my father's business as payback. He's ruthless and thoroughly without morals, and I dare say he hasn't improved with age. I hate the man with a passion. And I won't profile him.'

'You must be kidding, surely? You have right there the seeds of a brilliant profile!' The chairman peered at her as if he couldn't believe what he was hearing. 'I've never seen you back away from anything or anyone. What are you so afraid of?'

'I'm not afraid! I simply have no desire to ever see that man again.'

'Then consider it your chance to get back at him for what he did!' He slammed his hand on the table. 'Find the dirt on Alexander Koutoufides. He must be hiding something other than that sister of his. Find out what it is.'

She turned on him in a flash. '*AlphaBiz* doesn't do dirt—not in my profiles! Not that it matters, because I won't do it anyway.'

'You'd give up your chance at this promotion?'

'Why does it have to be him? Surely there's someone else I can profile?'

Sir Rodney harrumphed and drew back in his chair. 'I dare say the board won't be impressed, but I suppose if you feel that strongly about it we could possibly come to some arrangement. Perhaps we could swap your assignment for Carmen's?'

So she'd get Carmen's subject and Carmen would profile Alex instead? Saskia choked back her instant irrational objection. Maybe the chairman had a point. Why *not* set Carmen onto Alex? They probably deserved each other. Carmen would be only too eager once she discovered how good-looking he was—the perfect specimen on which to employ her famed horizontal interview techniques. And, let's face it, once she got him there Alex would have no reason to hurl Carmen from his bed—leastways not for the same reason *she'd* been so viciously ejected all those years ago!

Oh, yes, maybe they did deserve each other. She could just see it now… Pictures splashed across her mind's eye, shockingly vivid, staggeringly carnal, frame by slow, pulsating frame…

Carmen with Alex. Carmen on top of Alex, crawling all over him, over his chest, her mouth on his nipples, her hair tickling the firm flesh of his chest. And Alex, flipping her over, finding that tender place between her thighs…

Bile rose sharp and bitter in her throat.

Carmen didn't know the first thing about Alex! Whereas she herself *did* have a head start. She knew what the man was like, and she had a compelling reason, so he might just agree to do it.

Perhaps Sir Rodney was right—maybe this *was* her opportunity to get even with the man who'd destroyed her father's life and humiliated her into the deal? And maybe this was her chance to take Alex Koutoufides down a peg or two in the process.

'Sir Rodney,' she ventured calmly, in a voice that sounded strangely distant, as if separated from logic and reason. 'Maybe I was too hasty…'

He leaned his bulk across the desk in anticipation. 'Then you'll do it? You'll profile Alex Koutoufides?'

She lifted her eyes to meet his and swallowed, still half wondering what the hell she was letting herself in for and why.

For my father, she answered herself in the hammer of her heartbeat.

For revenge…

'I'll do it,' she said before she could change her mind again. 'When do I leave?'

CHAPTER TWO

ALEX KOUTOUFIDES was playing hard to get. Word on the streets in Sydney suggested he'd gone to ground, hoping to sit out the interest in his sister's latest affair. There was probably some logic in that, Saskia acknowledged as she edged quietly along the shadowy strip of sand lining the tiny and exclusive Sydney Harbour cove. Before too long another celebrity scandal was bound to knock Marla Quartermain's latest indiscretion off the front pages. Not that that would let Alex off the hook as far as Saskia was concerned.

But, with no sightings of him since the incident at the hotel, and no record of him leaving the country, Saskia had no option but to follow up on a hunch. Which was precisely why she was here, hugging the vegetation that lined the beach, contemplating the multi-storey beach house alongside.

The same beach house Alex had brought her to eight years before.

Saskia tried to ignore the steel bands tightening around her gut as she scrutinised the outline of the house in the fading sunlight, searching for any signs of life behind the curtain-lined glass walls. She wouldn't let herself think back to that night or she'd never be able to focus on her job. It was just a house, and Alex was just a man—not that it even looked as if he was here.

The garages facing the road high above had all been locked down, and there'd been no answer to her several rings of the gate bell. And she'd found not one reference to the property being owned by Alex or any of his known companies in any of her searches. Maybe it had never even been his.

Yet the strange prickle at the base of her neck told her otherwise, and despite the bad taste in her mouth at the prospect of meeting Alex Koutoufides again the thrill of the chase still set adrenaline pumping around her veins. It might be a long shot, but she'd won her fair share of industry accolades for stories that had resulted from her following up on just such hunches.

Alex obviously didn't want to be found. And if nobody knew about the beach house, then maybe this was the perfect place for him to lie low?

Her eyes scanned the height and breadth of the building, an architectural triumph in timber and glass, its stepped construction clinging to the slope behind as if it was part of it, and its generous balconies extending the living space seawards on every level. And from what she remembered the house was just as magnificent on the inside.

She jumped, swallowing down on a breath as a light came on inside. Because she knew that room. She'd been there, had lain naked across the endless bed while the welcoming sea breeze had stirred the curtains and the sea had played outside on the shoreline below. Even now she could recall the magic promise of that night. And even now she could feel the raw shock of Alex's cruel dismissal…

She squeezed her eyes shut, trying to banish those unwelcome memories. No way would she let herself relive the hurt he'd inflicted so savagely. She'd buried the mistake that had been her infatuation with Alex long ago. She was over it! Besides, right now she had more important things to think about. The house wasn't as empty as it looked. *Somebody* was in residence and she needed to get closer.

She flipped the collar of her dark jacket up, and checked to ensure her crazy hair was safely tucked under her cap—she was taking no chances that her honey-gold curls would give her away in the moonlight—before she looked back behind her, checking she was alone. But this was a private beach, almost impossible to get to, the steep path from the road barely more than a goat track. The shoreline was deserted behind her, the sounds of the wind moving through the leaves and a distant ferry her only companions.

Until the sound of a door sliding open pulled her attention back to the house. There was movement, the curtains pulled back, and she shrugged back into her cover of foliage as a lone figure wearing nothing but a low-slung pair of faded jeans stepped onto the balcony. Breath snagged in her throat. The light might be fading fast, but it couldn't disguise the identity of the owner of the powerful stride that carried him almost arrogantly to the balustrade. Nor could it hide the width of those broad shoulders, or the sculpted perfection of that bare torso as it tapered down to meet his jeans.

She lifted her gaze to his face, knowing she'd already had all the confirmation she needed before she even registered his features. But there was no mistake. She could just make out the stubble shadowing his jaw, his hair damp, as if he'd just showered, glossy and strong, framing his dark features and the chiselled lines of his face.

And inside her hatred simmered alongside satisfaction. She'd found her quarry. She'd found Alex Koutoufides in the flesh!

He shifted position against the railing and shadow and light rippled down his torso, stirring memories and comparisons. *In the flesh, indeed.* He didn't look so different from the way she remembered. His face might be leaner and harder, his chin more determined, as if he didn't make a habit of smiling, but he'd filled out across his shoulders, power underlined in each swell of muscle. Her eyes took all of him in, scanning him for changes, drawn to his chest and dark nipples, then further down, to where a whirl of dark hairs disappeared downwards into the soft denim that hugged close and low over his lean hips.

Those same hips had lain between hers. Those same shoulders had angled broadly above her as he'd positioned himself, preparing to take her…

She shifted, all dry throat and hammering blood, agitated with her body's instinctive feminine reaction and angry with herself for believing she could ever forget what had happened here so many years ago. She would never forget—*mustn't* let herself forget—not after the way he'd used her and abused her and stripped her father's company bare!

Saskia lifted her digital camera and fired off a couple of low-light photographs—just for confirmation. Sir Rodney would be delighted she'd tracked him down so quickly. How ironic that the place Alex had brought her to all those years ago, the place where he'd smashed her youthful dreams of love eternal to smithereens, had now put her in the driver's seat. It brought a smile to her lips as she stashed her camera back in her bag; there was a certain symmetry about it that appealed.

She'd get Alex to co-operate on this profile to give her the best chance to win that promotion, provide her with financial security and the means to take care of her father, or he'd pay for it with the publication of a few salient facts she was certain he would not want to be revealed to the world. Of course, the choice would be his, she thought with a smile. Unlike him, nobody could accuse *her* of being ruthless.

Right now he gazed out to sea like a master surveying his domain, one hand nursing a tumbler, the other angled wide along the brass-railed glass balustrade. Shrouded in shadow, she watched from below. Now all she had to do was watch for a chance to scramble up the hill and wait it out in her car. If he made so much as a move she'd know about it.

He turned his head her way and she shifted instinctively, aiming to get deeper under cover. But she stumbled on something solid behind her—a piece of driftwood. She managed to clamp down on a cry of surprise but momentarily lost her footing, grabbing onto a branch and rattling her cover of leaves while the driftwood skipped away down the thin strip of firm sand, rolling into the sea with a soft plop.

It was good to get some fresh air. The sea breeze on his face felt refreshing. The darkening ripples of the harbour were starting to sparkle as lights went on around the shore. The last few days staying here, with Marla constantly complaining about being cooped up, were really starting to get to him. But what choice did he have? The paparazzi were still swarming all over the Sydney office, waiting for him to put in an appearance, and there was no way he was risking letting them anywhere near Marla—not when they'd done such a great hatchet job on her already. He couldn't even rely on the beach house remaining secret, not now he knew all his records and property transactions were currently being raked over by every two-bit reporter in town, trying to track down where they'd disappeared to. As it was, someone had been leaning on the doorbell just an hour ago. A coincidence? Unlikely.

But they'd be out of here soon. All he was waiting for was the phone call to confirm they'd secured a place for Marla in a place near Lake Tahoe. Once inside the private clinic that doubled as a resort, Marla would be both safe from the press and entertained twenty-four hours a day. Tennis, massage or cosmetic surgery—the choice would be hers. By the time she came out the press would have lost interest. And maybe this time she'd manage to clean up her act for good.

He swirled his glass of soda unenthusiastically. What he'd really like right now was a slug of Laphroaig. The robust single malt would be the perfect accompaniment to the tang of sea air. But he'd made a deal with Marla and the house had been stripped of alcohol—he wouldn't drink if she couldn't. But hopefully tomorrow she'd be on her way. All that remained was to get her through the airport without being noticed.

His eyes scanned the surrounding beach. At least they were safe enough here.

The glass was tipped halfway to his lips when he heard it— the sudden rustle of undergrowth, the splash of something hitting the water. Instantly his eyes returned to the area below the balcony. An intruder? Or simply a possum skittering through the trees, sending debris seawards?

'Alex?' Marla called from inside the house. 'Where are you? What will I need—?'

'Stay there!' he barked over his shoulder. 'I'll be right in.'

He scanned the shoreline one last time before pushing away from the railing and turning for the door, sliding it home with a decided *thud*.

The breath she'd been holding rushed from her lungs. A close call. If the woman inside hadn't called out he'd have been bound to see her, lurking below his balcony. And skulking in the bushes was hardly the professional image she needed to convey if she was to convince him that she wanted a serious interview. She swung her bag over her shoulder and pulled her cap down low and tight. She'd acted on her hunch and she'd found Alex. Now it was time to climb back to the top and, if he wouldn't answer the door, wait him out. He had to come out eventually.

As for the woman? She clamped down on twinge of resentment—because it couldn't be jealousy—not a chance. Besides which, logic insisted it was most likely his sister he was protecting. Although the way he was dressed—or undressed…

She breathed out an irritated sigh. It didn't matter, anyway. It wasn't as if Saskia would have been the only woman Alex had brought here over the years. Whoever the woman was, she was welcome to him.

Carefully she picked her way along the shore. It was darker now, and the overgrown entry to the path was all but invisible in the low light. She was still searching for it when she heard the faint squeak of sand behind her.

There was no time to look around. A steel-like grip bit down on one arm and pulled, hard. She grunted in shock and tried to wrench free, but her feet tangled in her panic and she stumbled, the weight of her assailant behind her forcing her crashing down to the beach.

Breath whooshed out of her as she landed, her face cheek-deep in the sand, grains clinging to her lips and lashes, while behind her one arm was twisted high and tight. Pain bit deep in her shoulder.

'Who are you and what the hell do you want?'

His voice ripped through her like a chainsaw, and fear bloomed like a storm cloud inside her. Was it any relief that she knew her attacker? Hardly. Not when she knew the sort of low acts he was capable of. And not when he was hardly likely to be any more welcoming when he found out who she was.

She winced, her back arching and her head lifting from the sand as her arm was forced higher. 'You're hurting me,' she wheezed.

What the—?

Instantly he let go and eased his weight from her, horrified that he'd brought a woman down—but then he'd had no idea there was a female lurking under the bulky black jacket and cap, and whoever she was, she still had no right to be here. He crouched over her in the sand, not touching her, satisfied he didn't need to use any more force. She was going nowhere fast.

'What are you doing here? This is a private beach.'

She stretched her elbow, as if testing it, before planting it on the sand and using it to spin herself around into a sitting position.

Her jaw thrust up to meet him, and for a moment she was all pouting lips on a mouth that looked as if it wanted to spit hellfire and brimstone. He frowned, trying to make out more of the shadowed features of her face. She angled herself out from behind his cover and let moonlight hit her face, while at the same time she pulled the cap from her hair, letting her honey-gold curls tumble free. And finally those pouting lips turned up in a smile that came nowhere near her eyes.

'Why, I came to see *you*, Alex.'

And it hit him with all the force of a body-blow.

'Theos!' The word exploded from him like a shotgun blast, forcing him back up onto his feet. 'What the hell are *you* doing here?'

'I came to interview you,' she replied calmly, rising to stand in front of him and dust the sand from herself. 'But first I had to find you. Looks like I did.'

Before she'd finished speaking he'd already made a lunge for her shoulder bag and was rifling through the contents.

'Hey!' she protested, fighting him for control of the bag. 'What do you think you're doing?'

But he'd already found her mobile phone and camera and he ignored her, letting her snatch back the bag as a consolation prize. By the time she'd realised he had exactly what he'd been looking for, he already had the camera turned on.

Fury set his blood to a simmer as he scrolled through, finding the pictures of himself she'd taken from under the balcony. *'Vlaka!'* he swore under his breath, cursing himself for relaxing his guard for even just a moment. Just as he'd suspected—this was no innocent visitor! And now that *one* of the vultures had found them, at any moment the entire paparazzi contingent would descend upon them. Márla wasn't safe here any more. None of them were.

He flipped open the cover, popped out the memory card and flicked it low and long over the sea. He watched its trajectory over the water, only satisfied when it landed metres out into the bay.

'You can't do that!'

'I just did.'

He turned back to her, taking his time to really look her over this time—this ghost from the past come to haunt him. Little Saskia Prentice, all grown up. Sure, there were still those same long curls framing that heart-shaped face, the same too-wide mouth and milky complexion surrounding the greenest eyes he'd ever seen—but, from what he could see of the curves under that open zipper jacket, it looked as if the transition from teenager to woman had been good to her. Only the spark of innocence in those eyes was missing. Cold, hard cynicism ran deep in those liquid green depths.

For a moment he wondered—just how much had that been down to him? But he discarded that thought in a blink. No, her job would have knocked that out of her regardless. Nobody could stay an innocent for long in her line of work.

A line of work he abhorred.

'You're a reporter,' he said, pocketing both her phone and her camera in the shirt he'd hastily flung on before leaving the house. He hoped she wouldn't take his words as a compliment. They weren't meant to be. 'I suppose it's hardly surprising someone like you would end up working for the gutter press.'

'I'm a *journalist*,' she emphasised, her eyes now colder, her chest expanding on an angry breath. 'For a business magazine. And now that you've finished tampering with my goods, perhaps you'd care to hand them back?'

'And give you another chance at stealing one of your seedy shots or summoning up your cronies?' He knew exactly what kind of business magazine peddled the shots of the rich and the celebrated. He'd had his fair share of them. He'd seen how they operated—following their prey like vultures, wanting to make a fast buck by exposing someone else's private life. They were parasites, every last one of them.

'How am I supposed to do that? You've dispensed with the memory card, remember?'

'And a reporter would never carry a spare? I don't think so. Leave me your business card and I'll have your goods delivered to you.'

'That's my property! I'm not leaving without it.'

'And right now you're on *my* property, and I don't recall giving you permission to enter it—let alone take photographs you no doubt intend selling to the highest bidder. I'm sick of you parasites following Marla's every move, waiting for any chance to pull her down.'

'I wouldn't do that! Like I said, I work for—'

'Good,' he interrupted, not believing a word. 'Then getting rid of those photos won't present a problem. Now, who told you I was here?'

She looked at him, her hands on her hips, every part of her body taut and ready to snap.

'Nobody told me.'

'Then how did you find me?'

Her lips turned into something resembling a sneer, her eyes sparking resentment. 'Oh, I just thought I'd drop by on the off chance—*for old times' sake*. Surely you haven't forgotten that night? We had *such* fun together.'

Breath hissed through his teeth.

Forgotten that night? Not a chance. Though he'd tried to scrub his mind free of it time and time again, tried to put it behind him, his memory of that night was like a stain, indelibly printed on his psyche. It had been a mistake—an ugly mistake. And now Saskia herself was back, a three dimensional reminder of the mistakes of the past. What a fool he'd been to bring her to this house! And what a hell of a time to discover just how big a mistake it had been.

But, whatever she wanted from him, she was leaving. She was barking up the wrong tree entirely if she thought that what had happened all those years ago gave her an entrée into his private life now.

'I want you gone—now.'

'All I want is one interview.'

'You're wasting your time. My sister isn't giving interviews.'

'I don't want to talk to your sister. It's *you* my magazine is interested in.'

'Sure,' he said, shepherding her back towards the start of the steep path. 'Now, get going before I have to call the police and have you thrown out.'

She shrugged off his arm and stood her ground. 'I'm not going anywhere. Not without a profile on you.'

'And this is how you thought you'd get it? By lurking in the bushes and playing paparazzi?'

'I had to find out if you were here. You wouldn't answer the door.'

'Maybe because I didn't want to talk to anyone.'

'You have to agree to this interview.'

'Forget it. If you really had anything to do with the business world, you'd know I never give interviews or allow profiles.'

'This time you will. I work for *AlphaBiz* magazine—'

'Hang on.' He stilled in the moonlight. 'That's part of the Snapmedia conglomerate, isn't it? That bunch of dirt-raking parasites? I *knew* you were trouble.'

'I'm with *AlphaBiz*! It's a *business* magazine.'

'Closely aligned to *Snap!* magazine. Part of the same gutter press. And don't try and pretend you're anything special. I've seen the family tree.'

'You have to listen—'

'I don't have to listen to anything. Whereas *you* have to go. Right now.' He took a step closer, making it clear he wanted her to turn and leave. 'Goodbye, Miss Prentice. Be sure to watch your footing on the way up.'

She stood her ground, wishing she were taller, wishing she didn't feel so overwhelmed by his size and proximity, wishing his very heat didn't blur her senses and make her lose focus.

'You really don't want me to go, you know.'

'That's where you're wrong.'

'But if you don't agree to a profile I'll still have to turn one in. And I'll be forced to write it my way. Surely you don't want that?'

He scoffed. 'I have no doubt you'd work that way

anyway, whether or not I agree to this fantasy profile you insist you're here for.'

'I'll say how you assaulted me.'

'Go right ahead. You were trespassing—not to mention dressed like a burglar.'

She dragged in a breath, desperate for oxygen, searching for the courage to be able to force the words out. '*Then* I'll tell the world about the sick way you handle your business deals. You can say goodbye to being a recluse with the amount of media scrutiny you're going to get.'

He moved closer, looking down at her with the look of death he knew curdled the blood of any employee who stepped out of line. But she didn't back away. Instead her green eyes flashed up at him as if *she* was the one issuing a challenge. 'Just what the hell are you talking about?'

'I'll turn you from Mister Squeaky-Clean into a business pariah. Just as well you like living life as a recluse. Because you won't be able to show your face in public by the time I'm through with you.'

'You're bluffing!' he stated, even while a sick feeling foamed in his stomach, a festering of the unease he'd felt ever since he'd realised there was someone down below the balcony watching the house.

'You think so? Then watch me walk away. Because personally I can't wait to splash the sad truth of how you go about a takeover and exactly how you like to celebrate your victory by totally humiliating the opposition by seducing and then rejecting their innocent daughters.'

CHAPTER THREE

FURY turned his eyes dark and potent. His top lip curled with hatred as Saskia waited for his response. 'So much for having nothing in common with the gutter press. Looks like you can rake muck with the worst of them.'

'I'm not talking about raking muck,' she stated as calmly as she could, belying the fact that her heart was going at a million miles an hour. 'I'm talking about telling the truth, telling it how it was and what you did to me the very day before you destroyed my father's life by smashing his company to pieces.'

His face came down low, his brows twisted, his skin pulled tight over his features—features that spoke of barely reined-in rage. He leaned so close she could feel his breath on her face, feel his heat setting her own blood on fire.

'And what exactly *did* I do to you?'

'You took advantage of me!'

'So you're planning to pretend I raped you?'

'No! I never said that. Although no doubt you'd like to pretend we never had sexual relations at all.'

'We went to bed together, and you were, I seem to recall, more than willing!'

'As were you! Or so I thought.'

He drew back for a moment, his eyes narrowing.

'Is *that* why you're so angry with me? Because I *didn't* actually finish off what I started?'

She blinked, gulping back on a sudden spike of truth.

'Is that to be your threatening headline, then?' he taunted. *'Man refuses to take woman's virginity.* Are you trying to damn me or make me out to be some kind of saint?'

'Whether or not you stopped has nothing to do with it. You got me into bed, remember?'

'No,' he said, brushing her objections aside. 'I don't know how many men would have stopped when it was so willingly offered to them on a plate! You were all but *begging* for it.'

'That's not the point!' she protested, her stomach churning at the crude way he portrayed what had happened that night. Was that what he believed? Was that how he remembered it? It hadn't been like that. Not for her at least.

Suddenly things were too personal, too painful, his words slicing fresh wounds so that she had to battle twice as hard to overcome both the hurt of the old and the pain of the new. And so what that they hadn't actually had sex? It had been damned close, and his rejection had left her feeling violated. He'd used her for whatever sick purpose he'd had in mind, and then he'd hung her out to dry.

'Then what *is* your *precious* point?' Alex demanded.

'If it hadn't been for the takeover,' she managed, her words spilling out in a rush, 'you would never have had me in your bed. It wasn't enough for you to crush my father and his business. You had to humiliate the entire family in the process!'

His eyes flared and burned like a planet in its death throes, and she knew she was right. But there was no victory in his silent confirmation. Instead, the memory of that night ripped sharp and jagged through her senses as if it were yesterday.

She was back in that bed, her feelings as exposed as her flesh. Bewildered, confused and frightened of the man he'd suddenly become. Her feelings slashed to the core as she realised the fool he'd made of her. *The fool she'd made of herself.* She gulped in air, trying to think, to keep control, to suppress the pain of a night that should never have happened.

'You would never publish that.' His words were whispered and intense. 'You have no idea what you'd be opening yourself up to.'

She could hear the steady wire of warning running through his lowered voice, linking his words together like a threat.

'Try me!' she challenged. If he was threatening her he must be afraid—afraid of what she could reveal about him, afraid of what it could do to his business. 'The whole world is going to learn what kind of man you really are. And won't that do your precious sister a whole lot of good? Seeing you dragged through the press just like her! Goodbye, Alex. Sleep tight.'

She turned and he cursed, low and hard under his breath. Damn her! Just when he'd had Marla almost clear. Just when he was trying to keep her away from that gutter press, that same gutter press was about to turn on him. And there was only one way to stop it happening.

He snaked out a hand, imprisoning her arm before she'd taken two paces. 'Wait.'

She looked down at his hand, then over her shoulder at him, her eyes flashing like green crystals, cold and deadly. 'I don't like you touching me.'

He let her go, not wanting to touch her himself but drawn to her at the same time. 'What's to say that even if I agree to this interview you won't publish that rubbish anyway?'

'My word says so.'

'And why on earth would I trust you?'

'Do you really think I want people to know what you did to me back then? Oh, yes, I'll use it if I have to. But you give me this profile and I won't have to reveal to the entire world how much of a bastard you are and how much of a fool I was.'

'Then I'll give you your interview.'

She blinked, slowly, and his eyes were drawn to the arc of her long lashes, sweeping down over her eyes. But not before he'd caught a glint of something inside—success? Or fear?

But when she opened them up whatever he'd glimpsed was gone.

'Fine,' she said, almost as if she was sorry. 'When is a good time to make the arrangements? I'll stay in the background as much as possible, but you will need to allow for some one-on-one question time.'

'Hold on. I said I'd agree to an interview. Nothing more.'

'But—'

'And you've got ten minutes for it. Starting now.'

'No! That's not how I work. I can't be expected to do an entire profile in ten minutes.'

'So how long does a profile take?'

'At least a week. Sometimes more. It depends how co-operative the subject is. I need to see how you work. I need access to your offices.'

'A week? No deal. I won't even be in the country.'

Her eyes hardened into a renewed ice age. 'Then we have nothing more to discuss. It's a profile, or you can look out for what I write in the paper. And I warn you, it will be very, very good. Although perhaps not so good for you.'

The wake from a long-gone ferry slapped lazily up the shore, cicadas buzzed in the dark foliage, and all the while her eyes held his, daring him, challenging him to make the wrong decision.

Why the hell had she had to come back into his life right now? And with a score to settle. She was the last thing he needed.

The mobile in his back pocket beeped three times, and without moving his eyes he reached behind and put it to his ear, knowing instinctively that it was his number one fix-it man, Jake.

'Yes?'

He listened for a few moments, still watching her, satisfied to hear that by this time tomorrow Marla would be safely on her way to the States. Then what he heard made him do a double-take. 'What do you mean, "a diversion"?'

'The airport's still crawling with reporters,' Jake Wetherill argued. 'We can chopper Marla up to Brisbane and exit from there, but there's no guarantee that will be any clearer. But if we could pull something to get the focus onto you—hopefully Marla can slip through unnoticed.'

Alex's eyes narrowed on Saskia. 'A diversion?' he repeated, thinking wild thoughts. It might just work. And it might just help his cause in the process… 'You've got it,' he snapped into the phone, closing it down and slipping it back into his pocket.

Saskia eyed him warily as he allowed himself a thin smile. 'What was that all about?'

'You'd better come with me,' he said, taking her by the wrist. 'You don't have much time to get ready.'

'What do you mean? Get ready for what?'

'I mean you'll get your profile after all.'

She dug her heels into the sand, clearly not trusting him. *Clever girl.*

'What's the catch? What was all that about "a diversion"?'

'There is no catch,' he responded, pulling harder and forcing her feet into a jerky run to keep up with him. 'I'm just making you a deal. You'll get your profile, and in return you'll do something for me.'

'What "something"?'

He stopped, and swung his body towards hers so fast that she almost slapped bodily into him. He looked down and saw eyes that were wide and mistrustful, lips slightly parted, as if he'd caught her unawares and she was trying to catch her breath.

'Did anyone ever tell you that you ask too many questions?'

'I'm a journalist,' she argued, her gaze glued to his unbuttoned shirt, surveying his chest before backing up as if it might bite her. Her eyes drifted up to his face, widening when she saw the way he'd been watching her, waiting for their eyes to connect. 'It's my job.'

'And all I'm doing is giving you the opportunity to do it,' he announced.

'What do you want *me* to do?'

Alex looked down at her, at the moonlight playing on her curls and her body within humming distance of his senses, and for just one crazy moment he felt like sliding a hand around that slender neck and tipping those lips up towards his.

He must be mad to even think it.

Another time, another place—*another woman*—and that question could almost have been an invitation. But not with Saskia. If there was one thing he'd learned from his mistakes over the years it was not to make them again. Saskia had been one hell of a mistake, and he wasn't about to revisit it.

He raised his eyes skyward to break the contact, to break whatever it was she was doing with those damned green eyes of hers, and started pulling her towards the house. 'We leave tomorrow for the States—do you have your passport handy?'

'At my hotel. But the States? Why?'

'Does it matter where you get your profile?'

'No, but…'

'Then I'll send for your things. You're coming with me. You want a week; you've got one. All I'm asking is that you help me let Marla slip through the airport without being noticed.'

'That "diversion" you were talking about, I take it?'

'Got it in one.'

'So what am I expected to do?'

'Just accompany me through the airport. The press are still looking for Marla. I want them to find me strolling casually through the airport and holding hands—with you.'

He let the last two words sink in.

'You and me?' Her eyes flashed cold fire at the same time as her head started to shake from side to side. 'You want them to think there's something going on between us—that, what?—that I'm your *love interest* or something?'

He allowed himself a smile. She'd ejected those two words like missiles, and he knew he'd found the perfect person for the job. Whatever happened tomorrow, whatever he had to do to convince the press that they were a couple, there was no way she'd want to hold him to it afterwards.

'You must be mad!'

'On the contrary. It's the perfect plan. You get to accompany me and get your precious profile, and Marla escapes the country without a peep.'

'It'll never work. I couldn't… I mean, there's no way I could…'

'There's no way you could what, Saskia?' He slid his hand up her arm over her jacket, skimming over her shoulder, curling around her neck, watching her eyelids flutter in reaction as his fingers smoothed over her skin.

'Pretend you care for me? I think we both know that's not true. I think, if you think back, you might recall just how easy it was to care about me.'

Her eyes snapped open, but the rapid jerk of her neck didn't come close to dislodging his hand. 'That was years ago! There's no way I can pretend to like you now—not after what you did to my family. Not now I know what you're capable of. *Not when I hate you with every bone in my body.*'

'And yet you're here,' he soothed, his fingers gently stroking her skin, marvelling at its satin-smooth texture, feeling the rapid pulse of her heartbeat through his skin. 'Don't you find that odd? If you really hated me, why would you take this job?'

'I had no choice! Not if I want any chance at a career and a future. I certainly didn't volunteer to be here.'

'So you had no choice? And that's the only reason you're here?'

Something fleeting skated across her eyes, but still she didn't pull away. Instead she let her gaze focus, its power intensifying as she glared at him. 'No, it's not the only reason,' she hissed, her delivery gift-wrapped in venom. 'Once I knew I was coming I relished the opportunity to do anything I could to pull you down.'

So she really *did* hate him? So much the better. 'Sorry to disappoint you,' he clipped. 'So we have a deal, then—my profile in exchange for your co-operation on this?'

She nodded. Eventually.

'Good. Then, as soon as Marla is safe and your profile is done, you can take yourself back to wherever you came from and file your story.'

'Agreed,' she said.

'Just one condition,' he added.

'And that is?'

'You don't talk to Marla. Tonight or any time. You don't talk to her, and you don't take photos. Got that?'

Her green eyes flared into life again. 'I told you, I'm not here to interview Marla. My business is with you.'

His own regarded her coolly. 'Make sure it is,' he said after a moment, pulling her with him up the steps leading from the shore to the gate that led from the beach to the house. 'Or you won't know what hit you.'

Regardless of what Alex wanted, Marla was there to meet them as soon as they entered the house. 'So there *was* someone out there?' she said, her face a picture of curiosity, but Alex gestured her to stay back with a firm sweep of his free arm.

'It seems we have an uninvited visitor for the night.' Alex tightened his grip on Saskia's arm, his fingers biting into her flesh as if he was worried she was going to make a dash for his sister now she was so close. 'But I want you to keep right away from her. I'm putting her in the guest wing and she's not moving from it.'

'Who is she?'

'Just some reporter.' He spat the word out as if it tasted of bile. 'Nobody you need worry about—'

'I'm a *journalist*,' Saskia interrupted, sick of being talked about in the third person and conscious of how Marla had recoiled at the word he'd used. 'I came here to ask for a profile on Alex. I work for *AlphaBiz* magazine, and my name is—'

'Not important!' Alex interrupted, turning on her savagely, the look in his eyes enough to stop her in her tracks. 'And no matter what she says,' he directed at Marla, 'we're not taking any chances. Don't talk to her. And, whatever you do, don't answer any questions.'

Marla looked at her warily, as if Saskia might bite. Without the sultry make-up she was used to seeing the woman photographed in, Marla looked pale and vulnerable, her eyes wide and innocent, almost naïve.

'So why is she here?'

Alex was already leading her past Marla and towards a flight of stairs. 'She's going to help us get through the airport tomorrow in return for this profile she claims she wants. While we lead the way, Jake will look after you.'

'I don't want Jake,' his sister cried out. 'I hate him. I don't need a babysitter!'

'You'll do what I say!' Alex called back over his shoulder.

'If you expect me to help you both it might pay to stop insulting me,' Saskia hissed, as he frogmarched her up to a mezzanine level facing the sea, letting go of her only once she was safely deposited in a large sitting room.

He closed the door behind them while she rubbed her arm where he'd held her. She took in the rich décor, in coffee and cream colours with soft golden highlights, and guessed the closed curtains must be hiding spectacular views of the harbour. Through an open door she could make out a bedroom, the large bed and enormous pillows reminding her of another bed in this house, another time… She jerked her eyes away, heat filling her cheeks.

He hadn't brought her here to continue where he'd left off. *Besides which, there wasn't a snowball's chance in hell she'd let him.*

'I don't want you leaving these rooms. I'll send up something for you to eat.'

'So I'm to be your prisoner here, in this—' she swung her arms out wide '—gilded cage?'

His eyes were hooded and dark, his delivery deadpan.

'You'll find you have everything you need. There's an *en suite* bathroom off the bedroom. You'll have no need to leave.'

'I need my luggage. And I have a rental car to return. I can't do either of those if I'm stuck here.'

'Give me your keys. I'll have everything taken care of.'

'I don't want someone else poking around in my things! I want to get them.'

'You're not going anywhere. Not until tomorrow. Until then you're going to do everything I say.'

'Do you get off on bossing around women, telling them what they can and cannot do? Even your own sister isn't allowed to decide who she speaks to or who she travels with.'

'Leave my sister out of this!'

'I wouldn't take that kind of treatment if I had a brother. I'm surprised she puts up with it. I'd tell you well and truly where to get off.'

A pointed hand spun close to her face. 'And I said it's none of your concern! You know nothing about it and you will stay out of it. Have you got that?'

She regarded the hand levelly. 'What I've got is that it wouldn't matter if she *did* complain about your interference. You probably wouldn't listen anyway.'

'For someone who claims not to be interested in my sister, you sure seem to be pretty focused on her right now.'

'Don't you think it's a bit hard when you're making me stay in the same damned house as her? It's not as if she's invisible!'

He spun around. 'You're here for one purpose, and one purpose only—to ensure that Marla gets through the airport without the paparazzi getting wind of it. Do that and you get all the time you want to do this profile you claim you need. Otherwise, no deal. Have you got that?'

'Oh, loud and clear,' she replied. 'But don't you forget—

one wrong move on your part and I'll write an exposé that's going to set your business back years.'

His eyes sparked white-hot and his face took on a rigidity that could challenge concrete. For a moment she felt the heated resentment pulsate across the distance from him in rolling waves. And then something else crossed his eyes and he smiled, all tight lips and sardonic pleasure. 'I'm so glad we understand one another. Your things will be delivered later. Until then, goodnight.'

Sydney's international terminal was buzzing when the black stretch limousine pulled up outside the departures gates. Saskia took a deep breath as she waited for the chauffeur to come around and open the door, trying to prepare herself for her role as Alex's love interest. *Love interest?* Ha! After the way he'd treated her last night she'd have more success playing his hate interest. But with any luck nobody would notice them, and she'd get away with little more than having to hold his hand as they walked through the terminal—though even the thought of touching him was abhorrent to her.

Then she stole a glance at the man at her side and swore a silent *No chance* in her brain. If it wasn't enough of a sign-board to get the longest stretch limo in Sydney, nobody could miss a man of Alex's stature and bearing. And if his dark looks, the Hugo Boss jacket, the fine wool sweater and dark trousers weren't enough, he wore power like a magnet, and it drew people's attention from all directions. And wasn't this whole exercise about being noticed? She was wishing for the impossible.

Alex alighted first and turned back, extending one hand towards her, sunglasses obscuring his eyes. 'Ready?' She'd thought she was, but having him waiting for her, holding his hand out to her in invitation, made her hesitate and catch her breath again as she reminded herself exactly why she was playing along with him.

Just for show, she told herself. *Just for my profile and then I'm gone.*

Saskia reached up a hand, doing her best to ignore the warm tingling rush to her skin as he folded his long fingers around hers, the pressure gentle and firm as he led her from the car. A late summer breeze caught at her curls and the silk chiffon layers of her dress as he drew her close alongside, and with only one free hand it was her hair that came off second best. Even in an atmosphere rich with traffic fumes bouncing around the sun-warmed concourse, it was his scent of which she was most aware, his cologne that teased her nostrils, his masculine warmth that curled its way inside her and did unwanted things to her heart-lung function.

She looked around nervously, trying to take her mind off the man at her side while the chauffeur unloaded their luggage onto a trolley. It seemed to be taking an inordinately long time. But that was no doubt for the press's benefit—to given anyone in the airport time to realise exactly who had just descended upon them. Already heads were turning their way, a palpable buzz of conjecture vying with the constant roar of vehicles. She looked back down the approach lane, knowing that a dozen cars back sat Marla, a brunette bob hiding her trademark bleached silver blonde mane, and a burgundy leisure suit dressing down a body usually more scantily clad. Jake was at her side, both of them waiting for Alex and Saskia to draw any unwanted attention from the press and allow them a clear run through check-in to the relative anonymity of the first-class lounge.

'Do you realise just how beautiful you look today?'

His words snapped her head around and up with a jolt, but neither his dark-shaded eyes nor the firm set of his chin added to the effect of the words. Part of the act, she realised, damping down her erratically beating heart. Besides which, she didn't give a damn what he thought. But then his free hand smoothed the hair she'd been unable to rescue from the wind, curving it behind one ear and lingering there, all gentle touch and potent masculinity at the same time, making a mockery of all her efforts at controlling her crazy heart-rate.

She mustn't let him affect her this way! Once upon a long time ago she had, and it had been the biggest mistake of her life. And yet still, in spite of all she'd experienced and all she knew, he had a knack of getting under her skin.

He'd driven her to frustration this morning, making her change twice before despairing of the serviceable suits and blouses she had in her luggage and ordering in a boutique's worth of outfits and shoes for her to choose from. And even then he hadn't trusted her. He'd selected the dress she was wearing—a confection of fitted artistry and floating length, the muted petal print feminine without being girlish. He'd called in hairstylists, who'd transformed her unruly curls into sleek waves. He'd made her into a woman he'd be prepared to be photographed alongside, and she had to admit she liked the effect. She felt good—better than good—she actually felt beautiful. It didn't help that his words mirrored her own thoughts. It helped even less that his touch magnified what she felt tenfold.

She moved to shrink away from his reach, but he stilled her by placing one hand on her shoulder. 'Easy,' he murmured, his mouth so close that his warm breath fanned her face, sending tiny tremors radiating through her. 'We want this to look convincing.' And then he slid his sunglasses from his face, laughing softly, as if sharing some intimacy, looking down at her as if she was the only thing on earth that mattered to him. A panicked feeling of *déjà-vu* clawed at her fragile insides.

She knew those eyes. She knew what they could do and how they could turn on the heat and the desire and the want. She also knew exactly how easily those eyes could turn savage and cold in an instant, slashing through her soul with ruthless efficiency.

I can't do this.

As if on cue his eyes turned hard and resolute, and instantly she knew she'd unconsciously given voice to her thoughts. 'You *have* to do this,' he ordered, snapping her out of her fears as he steered her towards where their luggage was being wheeled into the terminal. 'We have a bargain.'

She blinked, her mind clearing now that it was passengers and luggage and queues that filled her vision rather than his eyes. He was right. She *could* do this. She had to, because she had no choice. But this time she'd make sure she had nothing to fear.

Because knowledge was power. This time it would be different, because she knew exactly what kind of man Alex Koutoufides was. She knew how he could turn on the charm, and she knew how he could so quickly spin that setting to deep freeze.

So there was no way she'd let him get the better of her.

They hadn't taken half a dozen steps inside the terminal when it started—a swelling hubbub of interest and more swivelled heads. Even though first-class check-in was fast and efficient, the attendant the soul of discretion as he checked their bags, by the time they'd received seat allocations and turned towards the departure lounges they'd attracted every eye in the terminal along with a clutch of photographers, both amateur and professional, who had suddenly appeared out of the woodwork.

'Here come the vultures,' Alex said, taking her arm and ignoring the calls starting to come from the photographers to attract his attention. 'Let's go.'

He didn't wait for her agreement, just forged a path through security as the gathering throng formed an honour guard around them.

'How's Marla?' someone called.

'Where is she?' yelled another, thrusting a tiny microphone into his face.

Alex brushed it away, tossing a pointed, 'I was hoping you could tell me,' at them. 'You seem to know everything else about her,' he finished, while he continued to part the sea of reporters and intrigued bystanders in his path as if they weren't there.

Saskia kept up, swept along as much by Alex's powerful aura as his arm around her shoulders. The noise of the incessant questions, the flash of cameras and the closeness of the press was claustrophobic. No wonder he'd wanted to protect Marla from this sort of circus.

Over the sea of heads and raised cameras the promise of the first-class lounge access appeared, and then disappeared behind them as Alex forged on, irrationally forgoing privacy for a public lounge setting at a cosy bar nearby.

What the hell was he thinking? she thought as he pulled her down alongside him, wrapping a possessive arm around her shoulders.

'So who's the lady friend?' one intrepid reporter asked, obviously tiring of getting no answers about Marla and determined to get at least some copy to file and make today's expedition worthwhile. 'It's not often we get to see Australia's most eligible bachelor, let alone with a woman in tow.'

Like a barometer, his comment was indicative of a change

in the mood of the audience and instantly attention switched from Marla to Saskia. Any story was apparently better than none. Alex smiled at her as he turned from the waitress who'd taken his order for the best French champagne.

'No comment,' he said.

The reporters took the bait, focusing now on Saskia, hitting her with a barrage of questions, each indiscernible from the next. Saskia recoiled from the push of people and microphones, everything and everyone in her face, her eyes blinking at the never-ending flash of cameras, her heart thumping like a cornered rabbit, powering an urge to jump up and flee.

Alex held up one hand to quieten the mob while he took her hand in the other. 'Saskia is a good friend, nothing more.'

But the look he shot her for the benefit of the cameras was pure sin, hot with desire and so heavy with lust that even Saskia caught her breath as his eyes triggered an instantaneous feminine rush of hormones inside her. Under her wisp of a bra her breasts tingled, her nipples firmed and peaked, and electricity crackled from their aching tips all the way down to her core. She dredged up a smile in response as she clamped down on muscles suddenly making their unwelcome presence felt, battling to rein in her inner hormones. It was merely part of the act, she reminded herself stiffly, as the cameras went mad amidst more calls for details.

She smiled enigmatically for the cameras. At least she'd soon be out of here—her mission accomplished. Marla and Jake should have made it through to the first-class lounge by now, and thankfully her part in this charade would soon be over, with the press convinced she was some kind of girlfriend and totally unaware that by the time they reported it the big news affair would already be over.

'Maybe we should tell them after all, sweetheart?'

His words pulled her around, aghast. *Sweetheart?* Tell them *what?* Cold chills worked down her back and she knew she couldn't run now if she tried—her spine had turned to jelly, her legs would cave at the first step.

'Alex?' she whispered, looking for him to reassure her that this game was nearly over, even though her gut instinct told her that Alex was hardly the kind of man to suddenly turn from dragon into knight in shining armour.

'I know, I know,' he countered, still holding his other palm up as he nestled closer to her, his leg brushing against hers from hip to knee. Heated. Arousing.

Irritating.

'I know we meant to keep it just between ourselves for a little while longer.'

'Keep what between yourselves, Mr Koutoufides?' Reporters jostled for the best position, sensing a major announcement. 'So the lady's more than just a good friend?'

Saskia felt a roiling wave of panic course through her. What the hell was he playing at? She'd kept her end of the deal. Hadn't she done enough? She forced a smile to her face, leaned into his shoulder, and hissed, 'This isn't what we planned!'

He tugged her closer into the crook of his shoulder and pressed his lips to her hair. 'I know that, darling. But why wait?' He paused while champagne was poured, and ordered another half-dozen bottles so that everyone could join them in a toast.

'Gentlemen,' he announced, pulling Saskia to her feet alongside him. 'I'd like you to be the first to know. The beautiful Miss Prentice has just agreed to become my wife.'

CHAPTER FOUR

THE atmosphere around them descended into pandemonium as cheers from watching travellers vied with even more questions. The pack were pushing and shoving around them, angling for the best photo opportunity, but Saskia was almost oblivious to the noise. White-hot fury blocked out almost everything and everyone—everyone, that was, apart from the smug tycoon standing alongside her.

'Alex!' she said. 'What the—?'

He didn't wait for her to finish. Whatever she'd been going to say, his mouth crushed the words flat. Shock registered in her eyes, in the way she held herself rigid, and in the exclamation he captured in his mouth. He pulled her hard against him to mould her closer, slanting his mouth over hers. It made a good fit even better. Her lips were lush and moist, her taste sweet and strangely welcoming, given her history of antagonism. She might not like to think she was involved in this kiss, but her body sure was, a body clad in little more than fabric less substantial than tissue paper. And underneath that sweet floral print lurked flesh so dangerously womanly he almost wished he was somewhere a whole lot more private.

He growled his appreciation and felt a tremor reverberate

through her in response, melting her curves into even closer contact with him.

His mobile phone sent out a single beep and his lips curved into a smile over hers. Marla and Jake were safe. Which meant he could stop kissing her now, he registered, even as his fingers splayed wide through her hair, keeping her tightly anchored as his mouth continued to take pleasure in hers. The plan had gone well. He'd kept the reporters entertained, no doubt drawing in any reporters hanging back to see what all the commotion was about, and now they had both a story and pictures to keep them happy. It was a win-win situation for everyone—including himself. He hadn't expected to have found diversionary tactics quite so enjoyable. But now he'd done enough.

Besides which, if he didn't stop kissing her soon, he wouldn't be fit to be seen in public.

Reluctantly he wound down the kiss, taking his time, savouring the fresh taste of woman, lush and ripe, in his mouth. He cradled her head in his arms as he ended it, wary that she still might want to tear him to pieces. But for now at least her fight was gone, her lips plump and pink, her cheeks flushed and her breathing fast and furious. She looked up at him with those large green eyes and he saw confusion competing with anger. Any minute now that anger was going to boil over, and he'd have a hard time containing it, but right now she looked stunned, thoroughly kissed and very, very beddable.

Theos!

One look at her and the reaction he'd sought to contain resumed, unabated. He spun her in front of him and wrapped his arms around her slim waist, feeling her slight gasp of shock as he drew her against his firmness as together they faced the press.

'Thank you,' he said, over questions about where they'd met and whether they'd set a date. 'But now you'll have to excuse us. We have a plane to catch. Feel free to stay and enjoy the champagne.'

Somehow Saskia made it to the escalators up to the first class lounge, her anger rising faster than the metal stairs beneath her feet. And once the sliding glass doors behind them had slid shut she wasn't staying silent any more.

'*That* wasn't part of the deal!'

He smiled down at her, even though he was standing one step behind, his arms spread wide on the risers. If he'd wanted to make her feel trapped his body language couldn't have been any clearer. 'The deal was for you to pretend to be my love interest. I'd say we were pretty convincing on that score, wouldn't you?'

She felt herself colouring under the cold perusal of his eyes—eyes that had looked at her with such savage heat just a few minutes ago, eyes that had all but incinerated her clothes from her. And the heat hadn't been restricted to his eyes. Once his mouth had meshed with hers, once his lips had bent hers to their will, temperatures had been rising everywhere. Compelling heat. Tempting heat. Heat that had stroked her senses and massaged her sensibilities. Heat that had curled into her secret places until they ached with longing.

Only when he'd pulled her in front of him and she'd felt the unmistakable evidence of his arousal pressing hard against her, the shocking equivalent of her own body's reaction, had that heat turned sour, curdling the juices of her stomach.

Sickening heat.

What the hell was he trying to prove?

'Those pictures are going to be splashed all over the papers by tomorrow.'

'I know,' he said, as if he was delighted by the prospect. 'The gutter press is nothing if not efficient.'

'Do you really think I want people to see me pictured— *like that*—with you?'

'Right now, I don't care what you want. It was the means to an end, nothing more.'

'So did you *have* to tell them we were engaged? What the hell was *that* all about?'

'I had to keep their interest,' he conceded. 'I didn't want them drifting off before Marla was safe.'

'Well, you sure kept their interest,' she snapped as they stepped off the escalator into the lounge proper, waiting until they'd been welcomed into the inner confines and been shown to a private room before continuing her tirade. 'But there'll be another story soon. It's going to be the shortest engagement in history.'

'Maybe not,' he answered with a smile, gesturing her to sit in one of the deep club chairs or small sofas surrounding a central coffee table.

She gazed around, momentarily losing her train of thought. 'Where's Marla? Didn't you say Marla was safe? I thought they would be here already.'

His eyes narrowed and his whole face seemed to tighten. 'Do you really think I'm letting you anywhere near Marla? It was enough of a risk having you both in the same house last night.'

'But I told you—'

'No,' he said flatly. 'Marla's safe. And you're not getting anywhere near her. We changed the arrangements last night. Jake is taking her on another airline. Right now they're half a terminal away.'

'I told you, I'm not interested in Marla!'

'Then we're all happy. What would you like to drink?'

She threw herself back into the chair. 'You mean you haven't had enough *celebratory champagne*? I think you should explain what you meant before.'

He curved a lazy eyebrow as he gave his order to the waitress. 'Before…?'

'When you said this engagement might not be the shortest engagement in history. What did you mean?'

He shrugged, as if it was of no consequence at all. 'Simply that it might suit us both to keep this "arrangement" going for a little longer—at least while you get your profile done.'

'You're kidding! You must be mad! This is hardly an "arrangement". You made an announcement. You lied to the press.'

'And tomorrow it will be fact. The world will believe we're to be married.'

'No,' she said, shaking her head. 'No way.'

'You'll find a way,' he said, raising his swiftly delivered glass of Scotch to her. 'Or you won't get your precious profile. It's as simple as that.'

'We already *have* an agreement! I've held up my end of the bargain.'

'I'm just extending some of the terms, that's all.'

'You're reneging on the agreement, that's what you're doing.'

'It makes sense for both of us. Although we'll be staying at Lake Tahoe while we're in the States, I do have a fundraiser to attend in New York in a couple of days. You'll no doubt want to be there, to get something for your profile, and if you *are* there, given this publicity, people are naturally going to ask about our engagement. It will be far less embarrassing to both of us if we maintain the image that we're engaged at least while we're to be seen together.'

'You mean maintain the deceit!' It was unthinkable. There was no way she could act like Alex's lover. It had been hard enough today. And what guarantee would she have that he wouldn't pull another stunt like that? 'I won't do it. I've done what I agreed to do. It's time to hold up your end of the bargain.'

He shrugged. 'That's too bad. Because if you won't do it, you won't be getting your profile.'

Blood pumped so hot and fast through her veins that she could feel it in her temples. 'Damn you! I should have known never to trust you. Knowing what you did to my father, the ruthless way you took over his business and crushed him, I should have realised you'd do anything to twist things your own sick way.'

His expression soured. His glass hit the table, slopping amber liquid over the sides, but he didn't seem to notice. His eyes were fixed on hers, his face filled with fury.

'And your father was such a paragon of business virtue? Don't give me that. He deserved everything he got. He *deserved* to be crushed!'

She stood up, her heart thumping in her chest, her blood pounding, outraged for her father who'd been destroyed by a ruthless takeover, outraged for her father who was now so ill and defenceless.

'How dare you? It's not enough to ruin the man's life and future. Now you have to stick the boot in with insults. Well, I've had enough of you twisting things your way. You can keep your profile, along with your phoney engagement. I'm telling the story I want to tell. You won't have to look for it—it will be everywhere—and it won't be pretty.'

'And what story is this?'

He sat back, his limbs sprawled over the furniture as if he owned it. The resentment was still there, but it was contained. And there was something new she didn't like—a smugness that irritated her bone-deep.

She looked around, aware that she might be making a scene, thankful that even if the noise of their argument escaped from this room the lounge outside was almost deserted, apart from a few travellers sprinkled around, either plugged into earphones, laptops or mobile phones. Then she looked back at Alex. 'I'm going to tell the world what you did—the way you crushed my father, the way you made a fool out of me.'

He only smiled in response, angering her still more, sending her hands clenching into fists, her nails pressing deep into her flesh as she reached boiling point. Her hands itched to let fly. Oh, to wipe that self-satisfied smile right off his face…

'This is a business magazine?' he said at last. 'Your *AlphaBiz*?'

She kicked up her chin. 'That's what I've been trying to tell you.'

'Do you really think the squalid history of your affair with the man you just became engaged to is going to be the stuff for business pages?' He waited a second, watching her, waiting for his words to sink in before he continued. 'On the other hand, maybe you could try to sell it at *Snap!* magazine. I hear they're always in the market for sordid tales. Perhaps they could use it instead of the pages they've got earmarked for Marla or some other poor victim?'

'But we're not really eng…'

Cold, chilling waves washed over her as the cruel implications of what he'd done to her today sank home. She had no story. Nobody would believe her now. Not once they'd seen the pictures of Alex kissing her spread all over the media. Why would someone who'd suffered such a shocking experience line up to marry the perpetrator? She'd be a laughing stock—if it was ever printed at all.

He'd painted her into a corner.

She'd been prepared to walk away from the profile, to walk away from her chances of promotion and a better level of care for her father—but only if she could have Alex Koutoufides's head on a platter. But now she had no chance of retribution if she took that course.

Revenge would have almost been worth the cost of losing everything. But now, if she walked away from this profile, she wouldn't get a thing. No revenge. No settling of old scores for what he'd done to her father. No satisfaction.

And she'd be giving away all chance of getting that promotion and getting the kind of care her father needed.

'You engineered that whole engagement fiasco!'

He barely raised an eyebrow. 'Of course I did. Did you expect to be able to hold the threat of telling what happened in the past over me the entire time?'

She swallowed, trying desperately to think and knowing instinctively that bluff was her only hope right now.

'It doesn't change anything. I'll still show everyone what a calculating animal you are. I'll tell them the truth—that you engineered this engagement to cover Marla's tracks.'

'Who do you think,' Alex persisted, 'is going to believe you? Nobody will take you seriously. Nobody.'

'But what you did to me! I was only seventeen.'

'And yet, if it was such a terrible experience, why would you turn around and be prepared to marry the man who subjected you to this awful experience?'

'You bastard! This engagement is a farce.'

'But the world won't know that.'

'I'll tell them! I'll make them believe me.'

'And risk making yourself look even more of a victim? Everyone will assume we've had a lovers' tiff, and that for whatever reason you're feeling aggrieved and want to get your own back. I admit it will be embarrassing, but it will hardly ruin my career. Yours, on the other hand…'

He raised an eyebrow and casually crossed his legs, brushing off an invisible fleck of nothing. When still she didn't move he said, 'You look like you could do with that drink now. Why don't you sit down?'

'I hate you,' she whispered, her teeth clenched. But she recognised that she had no choice, knew that bluffing was pointless and that if she wanted to use this opportunity to get back at Alex Koutoufides she was going to have to come up with a new way. Because he had her.

She sat down, as he'd suggested, but that didn't mean she was through with telling him how she felt.

'I hate the way you treat people—using them for whatever sick purpose you have, bending them to what you need them to be. I hate the way you destroy people and their dreams without a second glance. I hate the way you think you own the world.'

Without expression he regarded the remaining contents of his glass before tossing it back in one economical slug. 'I think I preferred it when I was kissing you.'

She tried to ignore the swift, sudden zipper of sensation that wrenched up her spine. 'And what's that supposed to mean?'

'It's the only time you haven't been arguing with me.'

For a moment she was frozen into inaction. Of course the kiss hadn't meant anything to him—what the hell had she thought he was going to say anyway?

'In that case,' she snipped, 'remember it fondly. Because silence like that sure as hell won't be happening again.'

Saskia came to and jerked upright, her vague dreams of warmth and comfort dissolving as the black limousine slowed to a crawl and edged onto a driveway. She looked around her as the car idled, its driver waiting for electronic gates to open. Through them she could see tall straight pine trees, spearing into the clear blue sky, and a large stone residence rising behind.

'What is this place? Are we at Lake Tahoe already?'

'So you're finally awake?' he said behind her. 'You have no further need of my shoulder?'

She looked around in horror—was he joking? But the look on his face told her he wasn't. His position, so close, with his arm extended along the back of the seat behind her, told her that the comfortable support she'd felt for her head had been none other than the crook of his shoulder, and that the warmth she'd been dreaming about and relishing had been none other than the body warmth of the man she abhorred more than anyone in the world.

She must have fallen asleep some time on the two hundred miles of Interstate from San Francisco—although it was barely the middle of the day here, and the flight itself had been relaxing. Or would have been relaxing, she admitted, if it hadn't been for the dark cloud of Alex sitting alongside her, ignoring her for the most part, regarding her through guarded eyes for the rest.

And when they'd entered this car they'd sat as far as possible away from each other. Somewhere along the Interstate that had all changed.

'I fell asleep,' she said, immediately feeling a fool as she realised how unnecessary it had been to say that. And just as instantaneously she changed her mind. It had been necessary. He had to be made to know there was no chance she would have used him for support if she'd been conscious.

She looked out of the window to cover her discomfiture—nothing to do with forcing her eyes from his unshaven skin, the dark stubble adding another texture, another dimension to the chiselled character of his face.

'I realise that,' he said, as the car proceeded down the long driveway. 'Do you usually talk in your sleep?'

Her head snapped right back. She was afraid of the unknown, but damned sure she wasn't going to let him know it. 'So what did I say? How much I hate you?'

He shrugged a little, one corner of his mouth rising as he pulled his arm down from the back of the seat and adjusted his shirt. 'No, I don't recall that.'

'Maybe I was just getting to the good bit,' she snapped, refusing to be cowed.

'Maybe,' he said, as if he didn't believe her. 'Ah, here we are.'

The car came to a stop outside the impressive building. Stone, timber and glass combined to form a two-storey masterpiece. 'This will be your home for the next week.'

'I'm staying here?'

'More or less. I'm putting you in the guesthouse on the lake's edge. I thought you'd appreciate the privacy. It's self-contained, with its own study.'

The fact he'd given any consideration to what she might appreciate surprised her. Likewise his knowledge of the place. She'd assumed he'd rented the house as some kind of bolthole. 'This place is yours?'

'It's one of my properties, yes.'

She looked up at the imposing façade of the house. 'You sure don't do modest well, do you?'

'I've earned everything I have.'

'That's one way of looking at it, I guess.'

'That's the *only* way of looking at it.'

She swung her head back round to look at him, letting ice infuse her words so that he could in no way mistake her meaning. 'If it makes you feel better.'

His eyelids stalled halfway over his eyes. 'I'll let Gerard

drive you around. You can settle in, and I'll come and give you a guided tour of where you can and cannot go on the property in, say, two hours from now?'

She almost laughed. So much for his consideration of her needs. She wasn't being offered privacy; she was being locked down in her own quarters. 'You trust me by myself all that time? I must have come up in the world.'

Behind him the door swung open, as if the driver had instinctively known it was time. Cool high country air swept into the car, the fresh smell of woods and lake flushing out the strained atmosphere.

'Two hours,' he said, stepping out.

'I can hardly wait,' she answered, too low for him to hear as the car pulled away from the main house and continued down the driveway through the trees. As they turned a bend, her breath caught in her throat as the brilliant blue of Lake Tahoe, framed by still snow-capped mountains, extended for miles in all directions.

And there, nestled between trees on a small plot of land edged by boulders, sat what had to be the guesthouse. Like a miniature version of the main house, it featured natural stone, timber and glass set to take in the views that extended for the entire three hundred and sixty degrees around.

Without a word Gerard brought her luggage inside as she explored the cottage, and withdrew just as discreetly, stopping only to ask if she required anything more. If he was unused to installing women in the guesthouse, he certainly didn't show it. Although Alex's lady-friends were much more likely to be received in the main house, she decided. It was only untrustworthy visitors such as she obviously was who would have to be locked away in the far corner of the property.

Though what a corner to be stuck in, she thought, as she

completed her exploration of the two-bedroom, two-bathroom cottage, complete with study and, she acknowledged, as her eyes fell thankfully on the communication facilities, a telephone and even internet capability. Perfect to get this profile done as quickly as possible and let her get out of here. And perfect for the calls she should make to home.

Alex had been right about one thing—she did appreciate the privacy. Even if his motives for stashing her here were entirely selfish.

An hour later, showered and changed into fresh clothes, and ready with a portfolio of her best profiles she wanted to show Alex when he arrived, she hung up the phone after her first call, tears in her eyes. Her father had barely been able to talk—the result of a viral infection, his visiting nurse had told her. Although thankfully she believed he was on the mend.

But damn his cold, damp flat! No way should he have to put up with that any longer—she was going to pull out all the stops to see that she made this promotion, and that her father got the care he so badly needed. If only he hadn't been so stubborn about not moving with her into her own tiny flat and cramping her style years ago—maybe she could have prevented all this.

She swiped back her tears and collected her thoughts, preparing herself for her next call, expecting it to be only marginally easier than her first. She heard the extension being picked up an entire country and an ocean away.

'Sir Rodney—'

'Saskia!' His voice was gruff and urgent. 'You're in all the papers! The Board want to know what the Dickens is going on. I told them you didn't get along with Alexander Koutoufides, like you told me, trying to get you a bit of sympathy here. But now all of a sudden you've not only managed to track him down, you've obviously got him eating out of your hand. What are you playing at?'

'Sir Rodney, listen to me. It's not what you think—'

'It's utter madness, that's what I think. I was expecting a profile. Instead we'll be lucky to end up with a wedding invitation. After all the protests you put up about taking on the assignment, you're not doing yourself any favours with the board for this promotion, you understand.'

'Please listen. Alex Koutoufides and I are *not* engaged.'

'What on earth were you thinking? I thought you *wanted* this promotion. What's that? What did you say?'

'I said we're not really engaged. It's all a sham.'

'But the papers all said…'

'You know newspapers,' Saskia replied, irony heavy in her voice. 'Never believe everything you read.'

'Then what's going on?'

'It's a long story,' she said. *And much too painful to relate right now.* 'But I just want you to know that I'm working on the profile and you'll have it on your desk as soon as possible, as agreed.'

'Just as well. Because you know what's at stake if you don't. Carmen's already managed the impossible, and has convinced Drago Maiolo to allow her to do his profile, so you've got a race on your hands if you really do want this job.'

Saskia tried to absorb the news about Carmen's progress philosophically. Carmen's assignment was bound to be less problematic, without the complications of a history angle to work through. Still, she'd hoped for more of an advantage in getting Alex's co-operation—co-operation that now seemed suspiciously weighted his way.

'I do want that job,' she said.

'Then I'm sure I don't have to tell you how important this assignment is to both of you,' the chairman continued. 'Only one of you can get this promotion. I want you to put everything you can into it—anything that might give you an edge over Carmen. Maybe you can use this strange arrangement of yours to your advantage. Do you think this so-called engagement might give you a different perspective? Something you might be able to exploit?'

'No,' she stated emphatically. 'The engagement won't cut it because there *is* no engagement. It won't be referred to in the article. And as far as I'm concerned the sooner it's forgotten, the better.'

'Then what about the Marla angle? Is there anything there worth pursuing, do you think? What is their relationship? What's it like to be a corporate hotshot with an aging wild-child sister? Is he afraid her bad press will impact on his business? The board want you to find out. There's *something* there, given that he kept the relationship quiet for so long.'

She sighed. 'I'm not sure about that line of attack, Sir Rodney. I've met Marla, and she still seems fragile from that awful *Snap!* feature. And I don't even know where she is at the moment. Alex has done everything he can to keep me away from her.'

'Well, you know the situation there. But you really have to pull out all stops with this one. Carmen's after this job, and it looks like she's off and running. If you can capture both Marla and Alex in your profile, you might just get the edge.'

Saskia gritted her teeth and looked up at the ceiling while she considered her response. Damn this sink-or-swim selection process! Sinking wasn't an option any more. Not now she wouldn't be able to take Alex down with her. She needed to swim if she was to secure this promotion—and fast.

But damn it all that she'd drawn the short straw and been assigned Alex Koutoufides! Especially now, if the board was looking to interfere with the way she worked.

She drew in a breath, not liking what she was hearing. 'Are you telling me that's what the board wants in this profile—the Marla angle played up? Because I'm telling you Alex isn't keen—he's put up barriers the whole time.'

'Who's doing this profile?' Sir Rodney demanded. 'You or Alex Koutoufides? If you expect to become editor-in-chief, don't think you're going to get away from making the tough choices and doing the tough asks.'

It wasn't the way she was used to working, and she wasn't about to start now. Not that she was going to discuss that with Sir Rodney when he was already annoyed with her over this whole engagement fiasco. But somehow she was going to have to find a way, find an angle, to make this profile the best she possibly could without compromising her own integrity and still giving her the edge over Carmen.

'I understand,' she said. 'And don't worry. I'll do it. I'll get you the best profile you and the board have ever seen.'

'I'm counting on it!' he grunted, before hanging up.

She put the phone down, her mind still reeling from the last few days' developments, her senses still torn with concern over her father's sudden deterioration, and yet still too sluggish from changing too many time zones too quickly to know how to deal with it all.

If only there was some straightforward way out of this mess!

But she was kidding herself if she thought there was an easy way out. Alex's ridiculous engagement sham had killed her escape route dead. Now there was no way out but to go forward. He'd made sure she had no choice but to do the profile. And now, with Sir Rodney's words about Carmen's progress, she would have to make it better than ever. But there was no way she was going to stoop to using Marla as bait. This profile was about Alex Koutoufides, it had always been about Alex. And that was what she was going to get.

Saskia heard a noise behind her. She turned and saw the man who'd been occupying her thoughts standing in the doorway to the office, his face like thunder, his stance battle-ready. Her stomach plummeted. How long had he been standing there?

And how much had he heard?

CHAPTER FIVE

'YOU lying bitch!' He watched her take one guilty step towards him.

'Alex—'

'You liar,' he said, cutting her protest off, the blood in his veins surging and simmering into a crazy red foam that coloured his vision and crashed in his ears. 'All that garbage about wanting to interview me. All that rubbish about not being interested in Marla. Lies! All of it *lies*!'

'Alex, listen to me—' She took another step, but stopped dead when he started surging towards her.

'I knew it,' he jeered, coming to a stop right in front of her, so close that she had to crane her neck to look up at him. 'I knew you couldn't go on too long without showing what you were really made of. In spite of all your cries of innocence I knew what you were really after.'

'But it's not like that, I promise—'

'Is it any wonder I didn't want you talking to Marla?' he demanded, his index finger pointing damnably into her shoulder. 'You've obviously got the entire article scoped with—who was that?—your boss?'

'This profile is about you. Not Marla.'

'That wasn't your boss?'

She took a step back, then another, backing herself against the timber desk, swaying away from him as he followed her every move.

'It doesn't matter if it was, you have to understand—'

'Oh, don't worry.' He shook his head, the smile on his lips nowhere near reaching his eyes. 'I understand. I understand perfectly. You'll get this profile you agreed to. You're not sure how you'll get access to her, but you'll play the Marla angle up and you'll hand in the best profile ever. Isn't that what you promised?'

'Well, yes. But—'

'But nothing! You've lied from the start. You knew I'd never agree to let you interview Marla. So you thought that if you pretended to be interested in profiling *me* you'd get close enough to get the dirt on Marla. And you might have succeeded. It was a new angle. Nobody had tried getting to Marla via me before. And in spite of all my doubts, in spite of everything that warned me you were lying, I let you into my own home. I let you get close to Marla. And in spite of my trusting you, you let me down.'

'You never trusted me! Right from the start you've treated me like a cheat and a liar.'

He planted an arm either side of her on the desk, enjoying her desperation at her inability to shrink away from him any further.

'And is it any wonder?'

'What? Stop trying to take the higher moral ground, and stop pretending you let me into your home out of the goodness of your heart. You *never* trusted me. You only invited me into your house because you were too scared of what I was going to tell the world if you slammed the door in my face and afraid of what would happen to your business if you didn't!'

Her eyes were sparking green flame, her cheeks flushed, her

chest rising and falling rapidly, but all that mattered right now were those lips. Either fully animated and going at a hundred miles an hour, or lush and pink and warm when they finally stopped. *And he knew exactly how they felt when they did.*

'You're right,' he said.

She blinked. 'What?'

He scanned her face, watching her indignation turn to surprise, her eyes widening, her lips parting slightly, hesitant, uncertain…*waiting*.

He breathed in deep, inhaling the scent of her—a heady mix of one woman's clean individual smell enhanced with some fragrant lotion and all heightened by potent anger, *heightened by passion*—and he felt his own senses respond. He knew that scent. She'd drifted asleep in the car, her head lolling to the side, and he'd moved closer and thrown around his arm to support her. Only to have her nestle into his chest, fitting him as if she was made for it. So soft and trusting. So accepting. So different from how she was normally.

They'd stayed that way for at least an hour, her curves wedged tight and warm against him, her head tucked into the crook of his arm. And when she'd murmured something in her sleep, something indiscernible, he'd turned his face down to hers, thinking at first that she was stirring, and had felt her warm breath brush against his face, her lips so close, her scent so inviting, her body so warm and supple… But she'd still been asleep, her breath a warm promise against his skin, and as for those lips…

Right now he lifted one hand, unable to resist any longer, touching the pads of his fingers to the twin layers of their sculpted perfection.

'I said, you're right. I didn't want you to go public on what you knew.'

Her eyes dipped in one long blink, remaining still while he traced his fingers over the line of her lips, only the telltale flickering of the pulse in her throat betraying her nervousness.

'I didn't want you to go public on what happened between us.'

Her eyes opened and she swallowed, her lips moving under his fingers as the action in her muscles kicked up her chin. 'And now you've seen to it that I can't.' Her voice came across as rough and husky. *Sex with an edge*, he determined with some satisfaction.

He allowed himself a smile as he let his fingers drift lower, following the line of her jaw down to her throat, tracing the back of his hand down over the scoop neck of her knitted top. She shuddered under his touch, but she didn't pull away and neither did she lower her eyes.

'So I have,' he agreed, aware that his own voice had dropped an octave. 'So where does that leave us now?'

Her eyes were wide, the colour of emeralds sparkling back at him.

'It leaves me stuck here with you—trying for a different story entirely.'

'So maybe…' he ventured softly, '…maybe I should help you out with one.'

His eyes were dark seduction, his lips an invitation to desire. And when they touched hers barely, hardly at all, with just the lightest of touches, a switch flicked on inside her that sent her internal thermostat whirling and turned heated anger into a long, slow burn. She shuddered as his lips moved over hers, surprisingly tender, gently coaxing, achingly sweet, and her own lips could not help but accept his invitation.

So different from that kiss in the airport. That had been squeezed from her, stolen, wrenched from her like some trophy.

This kiss was like a dance set to the music of her beating heart, the rhythm slow and magical, mesmerising, evocative.

She felt one hand slide behind her neck, supporting her head as he deepened the kiss, his warm breath blending with his taste, his lips, his tongue seeking entry, gently probing, coupling with hers.

And it was, if the crust of the previous years had cracked and fallen away. It was like coming home. Because she recognised his taste, she recognised his touch. She let her hands do what they wanted, let them skim over his back, reacquainting themselves with familiar territory while his hands did the same, his touch so well-remembered, so cherished, so long missed. She didn't protest when he hoisted her up the short distance onto the desk. She made no sound other than to gasp when he cupped one breast with his hand and rolled one straining nipple between his fingers. She welcomed the way he found his way under her top so that she could feel his hand on her breast without barrier, his skin on hers. Compelling. Undeniable. Electric.

Was it minutes she felt him at her breasts? Or only seconds? Time expanded, each second filled with sensations too many to catalogue, too delicious to bother.

And then his hand was on her leg, shrugging away her skirt, sliding ever upwards, searing a path along skin to the place that wanted him, needed him, ached for him.

And when, like a replay of how his kiss had started, light and gentle and barely there, he touched her, she wanted to cry out with the bittersweet joy of it all. How many times had she dreamed this dream? Finding Alex the way he'd been, so caring and thoughtful and loving?

How many times had she longed for a repeat of just this special touch?

And now her dream had become reality.

This was the Alex she'd known. This was the way he'd made her feel. This was the Alex she loved.

No!

Her eyes snapped open.

Not loved.

Had loved.

This was the Alex who'd betrayed her.

This was the Alex she hated!

And yet she was letting him do this to her! His mouth was on her throat, hot open-mouthed kisses burning her skin, his hand pushing aside her panties, seeking entry…

She pushed hard at his shoulders. 'Alex. No.'

'Oh, yes,' he murmured, barely taking his mouth from her flesh.

She pressed her legs together, trying to stop him. 'No! Stop this.'

He levered his head away far enough to look her in the eyes, but he didn't remove his hand, continuing to gently stroke her in spite of the pressure of her thighs around him, continuing to find the sensitive nub of her femininity, issuing a challenge that he made it hard to overcome.

'Give me one good reason why I should.'

'Because I *hate* you.'

He allowed himself a smile. 'I figured as much. I could tell that by the way you groan every time I do this.' The pad of his thumb circled her, sending sensations shuddering through her, the barrier of her silk underwear no protection. She raised her eyes to the ceiling and dragged in a breath that was too full of the taste of him to fight. '*Now* tell me you want me to stop,' he dared.

'I—want—you—to…' The next word was nothing but a blur.

'I'm not convinced,' he replied with a low laugh, his fingers testing the lace edging of her panties, creeping beneath, undermining her resolve in the most potent way imaginable.

But she couldn't let him. Not now. Not ever. And breathlessly she battled to bring back all the reasons why.

'No,' she breathed, desperate. 'You have to stop.'

'Really? And why would that be?'

'You mean you've forgotten?' she taunted, with a shove at his shoulders, clutching onto the one thing she remembered so vividly from those days gone by. 'Because you "don't *do* virgins"!'

Alex drew back, allowing her enough room to escape from the desk and his confines to straighten her skirt and top, those words of hers jarring in his memory.

He'd told her that, he remembered. Was she still so resentful that he hadn't finished off what he'd started back then that she'd throw his words back in his face like that?

'So is this your idea of payback? Replaying a scene from years ago so it's you that has the upper hand this time?'

Saskia looked blankly at him, her empty stare frustrating him.

'Oh, come on. There has to be some reason why you'd pull a stunt like that. I mean, you're what? Twenty-five or twenty-six. It's not as if you could still be a virgin.'

She turned her face away. Too fast. But not before he'd seen the honest truth slice across her eyes, the hurt…

'Oh, my God,' he said, surprise fuelling an irrational burst of laughter. 'Who would have thought it? You *are*.'

'Don't make me sound like some kind of freak!'

Her voice fractured on the last word and she spun, her arms crossed, towards the wall. He took a step closer. 'I don't think you're a freak. I'm just surprised.' Very surprised, he thought, given her age and the kind of work she did and the people she'd mix with. It didn't seem the kind of work where you'd keep anything intact for too long, whether it was ethics, integrity or virginity.

But, notwithstanding her occupation, he was more surprised that someone as stunning as she was hadn't been seduced plenty of times, let alone once. Surprised and somewhat strangely, given the circumstances, even a bit pleased.

'Saskia?' he said, reaching out a hand to her shoulder.

'Don't touch me!'

She spun around to face him, her green eyes almost too large for her face, her lashes dark with moisture. But she was still coming out fighting.

'What kind of man are you? One moment you're accusing me of lying to you, of being here to drag Marla's name through the papers, and the next you've got me sprawled on the desk, pawing at me like you're some kind of animal.'

Her words sat uncomfortably with him, rankled with him. He didn't understand it either, but he sure as hell wasn't going to admit it.

'You're tired,' he said. 'Tired and emotional. Let's leave the guided tour until tomorrow. Maybe you should take a nap, and I'll have someone bring you dinner from the house a bit later.'

'Don't patronise me,' she spat. 'And don't bother with a meal. I don't want anything from you beyond one business profile. Nothing more.'

He felt a muscle in his jaw pop. 'A little while ago it was clear you wanted much more than that.'

She had the grace to colour at that. 'A little while ago I wasn't thinking. What's *your* excuse?'

* * *

Tahoe usually relaxed him. Even when he was working in his state-of-the-art office the lake and the woods and even the winter snows calmed him. It was a haven from Sydney and the office, but it was also a place from which he could rule his empire away from the day-to-day distractions of office life. It was supposed to relax him. That was the theory.

But he didn't have to look in a mirror right now to know that he was scowling as he walked back along the path to the house. Damn her. And damn his body's reaction. Though who could blame it? She'd been willing. So what was that she'd said about not thinking at the time? Hell, how much thinking was involved in knowing you wanted someone? It wasn't *University Challenge*.

What was it about her that made him want to forget why he shouldn't touch her—and why he shouldn't want to?

The portfolio she'd thrust into his hands before he'd departed slapped against his leg. He lifted it, regarding its burgundy cover critically. Did she really think a collection of her pieces was going to make a difference to anything now? Not a chance.

The morning was crystal clear, the air so chilled from both the elevation and the remnants of the season's snow that her breath turned to fog as she walked along the boulder-strewn shoreline. Saskia hugged her jacket closer around her and wandered out along the timber pier built into the water.

It was early, not long after dawn, but she hadn't been able to stay in bed. Her body clock was out of whack. Before her the lake stretched miles in every direction, the surface of the water almost polished smooth. Two ducks glided effortlessly across the small bay, their wake the only disturbance to the mirror-like finish of the water.

It was beautiful here. The water so clear she could see the rock-strewn sand below, the air so clean it hurt. If it wasn't for Alex she might almost imagine enjoying her stay.

'You're up early.'

She jumped and spun around. A woman stood on the shore, watching her, her hands deeply buried in her jacket pockets, her face framed with the fluffy fur lining of her hood. But she still recognised her immediately.

'Marla. I didn't hear anyone coming.'

The woman walked towards her, her fancy pink western boots clomping as she sashayed up onto the wooden deck. She stood alongside Saskia, took a deep breath and looked around. 'I just love it here,' she said, smiling. 'It's my favourite place in the world.'

'I didn't realise you were staying here.'

'I wasn't supposed to be. Alex had me booked into a clinic nearby, but I refused point-blank to go. I can't stand the kind of people they get in those places. Desperate movie stars, failed musicians—the whole nip and tuck set. *Ugh*. Don't get me wrong—I know I'm far from perfect, and I like a margarita just as much as the next girl—well…' She smiled conspiratorially and a little sadly and conceded, '…maybe just a tad more. But I know that if anyone makes me go to group therapy one more time I'm going to throw up.'

Saskia laughed for the first time in what seemed like for ever, and then looked over her shoulder self-consciously to where the house loomed up on one side. Could anyone see them down here?

'I'm not supposed to have anything to do with you, you know.'

'I know. Alex told me the same thing.' She pulled a manicured hand from a pocket and placed it on Saskia's, her eyes as brilliant a blue as the ice-cold depths of the lake. 'But I get so tired of being told what to do. Don't you?'

Oh, yes, she thought with a vengeance. But I need this profile. Otherwise things might be different.

'He doesn't trust me,' she told Marla by way of explanation. 'He thinks I want to do some sort of exposé on you.'

Marla laughed, throwing her head up high, and putting her hand back in her pocket. 'My brother is the consummate Mediterranean man—even though our mother was a true-blue Australian. He takes after his father and he doesn't trust anyone, let alone anyone from the press. I have to say I've given him fairly good cause to be wary over the past few years. He's probably entitled to a little paranoia.'

'So you're not worried I'm here to get the scoop on you?'

Marla shook her head. 'If you really wanted to interview me I figure you would have found a way before now. I'll risk it. Besides, I wanted to thank you.'

'Whatever for? Helping you get through the airport?'

'Partly. You don't know what a drag it is not to be able to move without cameras being stuck in your face.'

Saskia grimaced, remembering the melee at the airport. 'Oh, I think I have some idea. I'd hate it, I know.'

'But I really wanted to say thanks for whatever it is you're doing to Alex. You've really got under his skin—I expected more of a fight last night over my refusing to go to the clinic, but it's like he's lost focus. For once he's not permanently on my case. Thanks for taking the heat off me for a while.'

Saskia studied the almost perfect reflection of the trees and the mountains in the lake while she mulled over Marla's words. Alex certainly hadn't lacked any focus yesterday when he'd come on to her. Quite the contrary.

'You know he's told the press we're engaged?'

'Oh, God, I know. It's even made it into the papers here. Haven't you seen? I can get some papers sent over to the guesthouse.'

'Thanks all the same,' Saskia replied. 'But I really don't think I want to see them.'

They stood together at the end of the small pier, silently watching the sun lift over the mountains on the eastern side of the lake, until finally Marla sighed. 'I'd better get back before Jake returns from the gym, notices me missing and puts out an APB. That man really is driving me crazy. Will I see you tomorrow morning, before you leave for New York?'

It took a moment for Saskia to make the connection.

'Oh, you mean the fundraiser? Alex mentioned something before our flight here.' She shook her head. 'But I don't know any of the details.'

'He's taking you to show off as his new fiancée—another exercise in calling the press dogs off me. He's determined to take his brotherly obligations seriously, it seems. I guess I ask for it. It must be a real drag having a middle-aged sister who's totally unemployable and who's got no talent other than to get herself photographed in the most embarrassing predicaments with the worst guys she possibly could.'

'Oh, come on. You're too hard on yourself.'

Marla raised her perfectly sculpted eyebrows, but the ironic smile on her face looked genuine enough.

'Thanks. You're sweet, but I'm not too stupid to realise my own failings. Even though the press like to make more of them than they really are.' She looked up sharply. 'Oh, I didn't mean you.'

'I know,' Saskia conceded with a smile, surprised to find she liked Alex's sister so much. She hadn't expected to. With her bad press, and with her brother's rabid defence of her, she hadn't known what to expect.

'I really have to go, but I'll look out for you here tomorrow morning. It's so nice to have another woman to talk to for a change. And, Saskia?'

'Yes?'

'Do you think you could do a favour for me?'

'Sure.' She shrugged. 'If I can. What is it?'

Marla hesitated, her smile sheepish. 'Do you know anything about publishing—I mean book publishing?'

Saskia surveyed the woman suspiciously. 'Well, a little. I did do one writing unit in my business degree and I've got some connections in the industry. Why?'

The older woman had a hopeful expression. 'A friend of mine wrote down some stories—sort of snippets of her life in anecdotes, nothing fancy. I read it, but I really don't know if it's any good. Do you think you could look it over for her? Maybe even pass it on to someone if it's any good?'

Saskia didn't flinch, even though every cell was on red alert. 'For your *friend*?'

Marla nodded, her blue eyes large and pleading. 'She'd really appreciate it. Please? I'll bring it tomorrow morning, same time, if that's okay?'

'I'm not sure,' Saskia offered in response, not falling for that 'friend' story for an instant. 'I don't think Alex would like it.'

'Please?' Marla implored. 'It's so important to her. And he doesn't have to find out. It'll be our little secret. And it would make my friend so happy.'

She looked so hopeful, almost desperate, and Saskia felt for her. It couldn't be easy being Alex's sister, despite her wealth and creature comforts.

'Of course I will,' she relented, watching the other woman's expression turn to delight even while knowing she must be mad to even consider it. Whatever that book contained, it could be pure dynamite in the wrong hands. If Alex so much as got wind of what she was doing she'd be dead meat.

Which meant she'd just have to make sure he didn't.

CHAPTER SIX

ALEX KOUTOUFIDES was not in a good mood. He couldn't blame it on the weather—at thirty-five thousand feet above the clouds the sun shone in a perfect azure sky as the private jet tracked to New York City. And for once he couldn't blame it on Marla. This morning she'd seemed happier than she had in years, her eyes bright and her smile infectious despite being 'locked away', as she put it, with her jailer, Jake. He couldn't even blame it on the fact he had to attend tonight's fundraiser. In the last few years he'd shunned all but the most select invitations to such events, but even the fact he was going to this one wasn't the reason for his deep-seated irritation.

No, the reason he felt so damned uncomfortable had much more to do with a certain file of articles he'd read last night.

He hadn't meant to read them. His intention had been to flick through and find enough evidence to support his prejudices before tossing the portfolio away, satisfied.

But that hadn't happened. His dismissive flick through had become hijacked by the very first article—a profile on Ralph Schneider, a senior member of the board of the World Bank, a man Alex had met on several occasions, and his interest had been piqued. Instead of finding the lightweight fluff he'd expected, he'd found the article in-depth and well researched, business information and facts balanced with a personal take on the man's character that Alex had found himself agreeing with. Somehow she'd meshed those different worlds to build a picture of a giant in business circles—a giant with a heart, and a giant you could trust to do business with.

But then he'd thought maybe Ralph had been an easy target? He was one of the business world's good guys, after all. He'd turned the page to the next profile—this time a billionaire UK property developer with a reputation for big talk and bigger buildings, and with almost celebrity status for his well-publicised charitable donations. Alex's attention had been riveted. He'd had dealings with a branch of this man's conglomerate back in Sydney, and there was no way he'd ever deal with any of his businesses again, after they'd cut corners on the contract and not delivered to specifications. Here was a man who would have tested her powers of perception.

But again Saskia's reporting of his business empire had been excellent, her coverage of the time she'd spent in his offices fascinating—and as for her profile of the man himself? Outwardly generous, she'd acknowledged, but, for all his popular media persona, definitely not a man to be messed with, and perhaps even one with whom to ensure more than ever that contracts were watertight.

It was a brilliant piece of journalism. There was enough in the article to make the property star feel good about himself, but there was plenty of subtext to make anyone dealing with him wary and cautious.

Alex had devoured the balance of the profiles, trying to find fault or a hint of gossip, but even while Saskia had taken measure of her profilees, she'd not touched on their personal lives. If they had mistresses—and he knew at least three of them who were so-called 'happily married' did—there was no mention of it. There was no mention of rumours of sexual preference, no hint of scandal. It was all extremely well re-searched and balanced.

In the end he'd flung the file away out of sheer frustration.

No wonder he felt sick. He'd accused her of wanting to get close to Marla. Time and time again she'd denied it, and still he hadn't quite believed her. But if the articles in that file were indicative of the kind of profile she intended to do on him, then he'd completely misjudged her from the start.

Theos!

He stole a look at her in the armchair alongside. Her eyes were glued to the window now, although she'd been busy for most of the flight, writing notes, or drafts, or whatever it was she was doing. What would she write about *him*? What would her profile say about *his* character after the way he'd treated her? It was hardly likely to be flattering. Would she stick to business, or would she be tempted to tell it how it really had been? A man who had promised her everything but delivered nothing? A man who had taken advantage and then taken nothing, and in doing so had left humilia-tion into the bargain? It was hardly the kind of analysis he wanted out there.

He'd rather not think about that right now.

Soon they'd be landing at JFK. Once this weekend was out the way and they were back in Tahoe he'd give her all the time she needed to get her profile done. And then she could go home, back to her life. Leave him to his. Let him get back to the way he liked to live.

But first they'd make tonight convincing. So what that Saskia wasn't interested in Marla's story? Plenty of others were, and the longer he could distract them, the more likely they were to let her go. He felt in his pocket for the object he'd removed from his safe earlier. He could put the profile off for a couple of days, but some things couldn't wait.

'Here—put this on.'

Reluctantly Saskia peeled her eyes from the window and the view of New York City coming into sight as the privately leased jet banked for its landing approach. They'd barely spoken on the way to the airport and through the flight—Alex seemingly locked up in his own thoughts. And if his mood was as dark as the glower on his face, she was glad he wasn't in the mood for conversation.

'What's that?' she asked as she turned, certain she couldn't have heard him properly. Then her eyes registered what he was holding and she plastered herself back against her wide armchair. 'Oh, no,' she said. 'I don't want it.'

'I'm not asking you,' he said impatiently, lifting the offending article towards her as if he was as keen to get rid of it as she was reluctant to take it. 'I'm telling you. You need to put this on. People will expect it.' She was still shaking her head as he continued, 'It'll be the first thing they'll expect to see.'

He was right. She knew it instinctively. But that didn't make the concept any more palatable. Pretending to be engaged to Alex Koutoufides was one thing. Wearing his ring, a concrete symbol of the promise they were supposed to have made to each other, of the vows they would make if this engagement had been anything other than a farce, was another.

Concrete nothing, she thought with derision. Concrete didn't flash and sparkle like these gems did. These diamonds would scream that she belonged to Alex Koutoufides—lock, stock and barrel.

'You don't like it?'

What was not to like? Its design was as masterful as it was spectacular. A large square cut diamond sat atop a two-tone band already filled to overflowing with a river of baguette-cut diamonds, flashing light and colour from hundreds of brilliant-cut faces.

'Does it matter what I think?' she snapped, knowing there was no point getting attached to it anyway. It wasn't as if it was hers to keep.

'No,' he conceded brusquely, his mood obviously not having improved recently. He reached for her hand before she could snatch it away. 'Not in the least.'

She swallowed as he took her hand in his, their palms brushing, his long fingers cradling her wrist. Why was it that just touching him set her temperature rocketing and jolted her heartbeat into double time? Or was she merely remembering the last time he'd touched her—and where he'd touched her—with those hands?

She must be shaking. His fingers suddenly gripped her wrist more securely. Could he feel her erratic pulse with his fingers? Could he tell how frantically her heart was beating right now?

With his right hand he slipped the ring on, gliding the gold and platinum band along her finger until it came to rest—an almost perfect fit. For a second he didn't move, just cupped her hand in his while in between them the ring sparkled and flashed, mocking them both with white fire.

'There,' he said at last, as if that solved everything. He let her go and sat back in his chair, his eyes closed while the plane made its final approach.

She lifted her hand, feeling the unfamiliar weight of the ring. 'How did you know?'

'Know what?' he asked, without opening his eyes or looking at her.

'What size ring to get.'

'I didn't,' he responded, almost as if he were bored. 'It was my mother's.'

Something squeezed tight in her chest. This was *wrong*! This was no quick purchase made on ebay. This was a family heirloom—an heirloom she had no right to be wearing.

'You can't expect me to wear this. Not your mother's!' She made to pull off the ring, but just as quickly he swung himself around and imprisoned both her hands in his.

'You will wear it. It's the ring she wanted me to give to my fiancée.'

'But I'm not—'

He moved closer, putting himself right in her face. 'When we're in public you are. It's expected of you. You might as well start acting like it.'

She tugged her hands out from under his. 'Fine. I can play the lovestruck fiancée. But let's not have a repeat of what happened at the airport. Pretending to be engaged doesn't mean you get to paw me in public.'

He glared at her, his charcoal eyes narrowing. 'If we're going to convince people that we're soon to become a happily married couple I'll do whatever it takes, and you *will* co-operate.'

The small jet bumped its way onto the tarmac and the engines screamed into reverse thrust. She knew just how they felt—having their efforts changed at the whim of someone who cared nothing but demanded all his machinery performed to his will. She felt like screaming too. But she was no machine. She deserved better than this constant frustration.

'I hope you're going to allocate me some time soon, to really get started on this profile. You've already wasted hours on today's flight, when you could have dealt with some questions I need answers for.'

He drew in a breath and let it out slowly. 'Where's the fire?'

Right now, it's boiling my blood! 'The sooner I get this profile done, the sooner I can get out of your hair and the sooner we can abandon this farce of an engagement you dreamed up. Surely that's what you want? But you've done nothing to help me yet.'

'I don't want to fight. Why can't you just enjoy a fun weekend in New York?'

'Fun? Pretending to be your floozy?' Saskia laughed, a laugh born out of frustration. 'I don't even know why you're persisting with this trip. I can't see that Marla is under any particular threat that you need to save her from, and our engagement story is old news by now. What are you even doing here? I can't imagine why they even invited you. I would have thought a fundraiser in New York was the last thing a known recluse would head for.'

'It is,' Alex agreed through gritted teeth, his indigestion getting worse by the minute as the plane came to a halt on the tarmac. 'Which is why it's so charming to have your delightful company.'

Saskia couldn't help but gasp as they entered the Starlight Roof of the Waldorf-Astoria hotel. If the grand marble rotunda in the entry foyer hadn't been impressive enough, the sight of the spacious art deco ballroom filled with tuxedo-clad men and stunningly dressed women stole her breath away. She'd been places in her career, accompanied businessmen and politicians while they went about their business in all manner of occasions and venues, but nothing compared to the rich opulence of this venue, with its two-storey-high windows framed by damask silks, its gilded ceiling and magnificent Austrian crystal chandeliers.

She gave up a silent prayer of thanks for giving in when

Alex had insisted on providing her with a gown for the evening. He'd already pressed upon her a closet full of clothes for their US trip, and she'd chosen from it a cobalt-blue silk pantsuit to wear—classy, but restrained, she'd thought. But this gown he'd had delivered to her room that afternoon, together with a tiara and a note that this was what she would wear for the evening.

The flash of rebellion she'd felt when she received the message had been short-lived once she'd taken a decent look at the over-the-top golden Oscar de la Renta silk taffeta gown and the diamanté studded tiara with it. Until then the cobalt silk suit had been the most gorgeous thing she'd ever seen. Now, looking around the ballroom, she knew that it wouldn't have cut the mustard. Not in this crowd.

It was sheer fantasy. A long, long time ago this would have been her deepest wish—to be seen in a dress such as this, on Alex's arm and wearing his engagement ring.

It was strange. She couldn't wait to get this profile done. She couldn't wait to get away from Alex Koutoufides and go home. But just for tonight she felt like royalty. Tonight she was a princess. And tonight she was here with the most handsome man in the room.

Why not enjoy it?

Alex tugged at her arm, wanting to get their entrance over. He hated events like this, though strangely for once he didn't feel so out of place. With Saskia on his arm, looking a million bucks in the gown he'd chosen from the shortlist Marla had come up with, for the first time since he'd begun attending the annual Baxter Foundation Ball he didn't feel the urge to leave within the first ten minutes. With Saskia to show off, he might even make it to twenty.

Cameras flashed in their faces, increasingly more so as

the reporters realised who they had in their sights. 'Mr Koutoufides,' someone called excitedly, trying to get his attention. 'Have you two set a date yet?'

Alex looked down at his partner who, surprisingly, instead of having to be reminded of her duty, he found beaming up at him, her green eyes sparking happiness and her lush lips turned into such a beautiful smile it completely blindsided him. Her hair was arranged Grecian goddess-style, topped with a tiara, leaving tendrils coiling around her face that he itched to wrap his fingers around to reel her face closer to his lips. If she kept playing the role as well as this he wouldn't make twenty minutes after all—he'd have her out of here and planted in his bed in under five.

As if sensing his hesitation, she placed a hand over his own—the hand bearing the ring he'd given her earlier—and the cameras took no time in focusing in on it as it sparkled and flashed in their lenses.

'As far as I'm concerned,' he said, feeling his own smile broaden, 'the sooner the better.'

Her eyes widened, her smile wavered, but she kept looking up into his eyes in that way she had, as if they were digging into his very soul, until he wondered once again if he hadn't done the very worst thing he possibly could by insisting she accompany him tonight.

And then the music started, and inspiration wiped out any regrets. Why bother thinking about the mistakes he'd made? Why think about who she was and what her father had done? Why bother beating himself up over things he couldn't change, things that could never be repaired, when instead he could simply take this woman into his arms and hold her close?

'Dance with me,' he said, taking her hand, already leading her to the dance floor. And silently she acquiesced, letting him lead her, letting him fold her into his arms as he drew her close and started moving to the music of the ten-piece orchestra.

She found her space in his arms as if it had been made for her, moulding to his body, moving with him like liquid warmth, and yet still turning him rock-hard.

He inhaled her scent, devoured it, letting it feed into his senses like a drug. Class and sweetness and lush, ripe woman combining in one package to make the ultimate aphrodisiac.

That number ended, the next began, and even the next after that. But still he didn't relinquish her. He kept her wrapped in the circle of his arms, drawing her even closer with every movement, until they were so close she rested her head at his neck. Their bodies were pressed together from head to toe, moving to the beat, moving with each other, until they were moving more to the primitive rhythm of their own bodies than the music of the orchestra.

Saskia didn't want it to end. She was barely conscious of the changes in the music, hardly registered when one number merged into the next, and then the next. If this was pretending to be Alex's fiancée, she'd volunteer for the job permanently. No pressure, no arguments, just the magic feeling of her body pressed up against his, the tang of his masculine scent winding its way through her, the feel of his arms around her, his hands on her—possessive, commanding, intoxicating.

The way he used to feel.

She could stay this way all night if he wanted…

'Saskia Prentice! I don't believe it.'

The familiar cultured girls' school tones knifed into her consciousness. She unpeeled herself from Alex in an instant, breathless and gasping, feeling the heat from every part of her body transfer to her exposed flesh.

'It *is* you! Wow, don't you look sensational?'

Saskia reluctantly blinked the last of her dreams away and plastered a smile to a face so obviously burning with embarrassment that not even the subtle lighting over the dance floor could save her.

'Carmen.' Quickly she recovered enough from her embarrassment to make the introductions. 'I didn't expect to see you here.'

Carmen smiled knowingly and took Saskia's arm, skilfully flashing the diamond lights of the engagement ring as she negotiated them away from the dance floor while raking her eyes over Saskia's dress in such a way that she could almost see the dollar signs ticking over. Not that Carmen's own gown was any slouch, wrapping her slim figure in form-fitting backless silver satin.

'Drago's just gone to get us some champagne. I'm here working tonight—just like you.' Her words might have been intended for Saskia, but her attention was now one hundred percent focused on the man at her side. 'Or maybe not like you,' she said with a soft laugh that made the ends of her sleek black bob sway with her glittering diamond drop earrings. 'I hear congratulations are in order? I didn't quite believe it before, but seeing the size of those rocks on Saskia's finger, and the way the groom-to-be looks at his betrothed, maybe there's some truth to it after all.'

Carmen raised one perfectly manicured diamante-studded fingernail and pressed it to Alex's chest. 'So this is the great Alexander Koutoufides,' she whispered huskily. '*Lucky* Saskia. Who says you can't combine business with pleasure? *I* always try to.' Her smile was too wide, her eyes sharp and pointedly bright, and even the provocative tilt of her body combined to suggest an offer.

Saskia couldn't ignore the blatant messages Carmen was putting out, even though she knew the woman too well to be surprised—if marriage didn't render a man off-limits; then a mere engagement would hardly register. No doubt she'd have a field day if she thought there was anything false about their engagement. She'd be all over Alex like a rash. Just thinking about it had Saskia's hackles rising.

Frustration, she told herself. She was frustrated at the interruption, frustrated at having her rival reminding her of the task at hand, and frustrated at being ignored by the both of them.

She was definitely not jealous. Why would she be? She had no designs on Alex Koutoufides.

Alex smiled in return as he lifted one hand and snared Carmen's, holding it closely between them before touching his lips to her fingers and taking an age to lower it to her side. Saskia knew, because she was counting the seconds.

'You're colleagues, then?' he asked, his full attention focused on Carmen's smiling face, on her delight at his gallant gesture.

'We are. Or rather we *were*. I assume we won't be seeing much of Saskia any more, though, now that she has such a handsome man to keep her busy? Such a shame. I was really looking forward to this competition. But I guess this means she's out of the race?'

'Actually, I'm still very much *in* the race,' Saskia stressed, sick of being excluded from the private exchange going on in front of her and silently cursing the arrangement that was threatening to railroad her chances of success. But she was stuck. She wasn't about to explain to Carmen the nature of her arrangement with Alex. The board were aware of the situation, and that was all that mattered. 'Our engagement changes nothing—'

'What competition?' interrupted Alex.

Carmen smiled up at him. 'Hasn't she told you? The editor-in-chief's position is up for grabs, and we're both in the running for it. Whoever turns in the best profile from our latest assignments gets the job.'

Finally he dragged his gaze from Carmen's and looked down into hers. His eyes were seemingly expressionless, and yet still she could feel them scanning for the truth, searching for answers. She blinked a silent affirmation when in reality she wanted to yell at him, wanted him to know *that* was why she was so desperate to get this damn profile started.

'I've been assigned Drago Maiolo,' Carmen continued, oblivious to the exchange. 'Ah, speaking of whom…'

A squat greying gentleman joined the party, his heavy-lidded eyes flicking over them, cooling as they passed over Alex but warming considerably when he came to Saskia. He handed Carmen her glass and immediately conceded his own to Saskia.

'I see you've found your friends.' His voice was almost as thick as his features, and it seemed to rumble up from below like an approaching roll of thunder.

Carmen smiled her thanks and nestled into his arm on a shrug of innocence. 'Drago told me Alex would be here. I figured you might be too.'

'How did he know?' Saskia asked.

'Alex is *always* here,' Drago replied, answering for her. 'He's been the major benefactor of the Baxter Foundation for years. Isn't that right, Alex?'

'Alex?' Saskia asked, looking for confirmation.

'How are things?' he directed to Drago, without answering either question, tension obvious in the firm set of his jaw.

'Never better. Especially now I have Carmen here to brighten up my nights. I usually have no time for newspaper people, but this woman is something different. I had no idea an interview could be so…stimulating.'

Drago and Carmen both laughed, even while Carmen

squirmed and redirected one roaming hand from low behind her. 'Drago's been most co-operative,' she conceded. 'It's going to be a fabulous profile.'

'It had better be,' Alex replied. 'Or you won't stand a chance of that promotion. I've seen the work Saskia does and it's excellent. And now, if you'll excuse us, I've just seen someone I really should talk to before the speeches get underway.'

He ignored Saskia's open-mouthed response as he steered her away from the couple, leading her up the stairs to the balcony above. She didn't know who was the more dumbfounded—Carmen, at being so thoroughly and cleanly put in her place, or herself, at first learning that Alex was the foundation's major benefactor and then hearing him actually defend her.

She looked around as he backed her into a quiet place overlooking the ballroom from behind a screen of potted palms.

'What are we doing here? I thought you said you wanted to talk to someone.'

'I do. I want to talk to you.'

Saskia recovered in an instant. 'Good, because I want to talk to you too. Did you really read those profiles I gave you?'

His lips curved into a thin smile. 'Did you think I'd made up what I said?'

She blinked. 'But you stood up for me.'

He shrugged, as if he hadn't given it any thought. 'I needed a line to throw her so we could get away. I think it worked quite well.'

'Of course' she said, feeling suddenly deflated that his support had meant so much to her and desperate to change the topic. 'So why didn't you tell me you were the foundation's major benefactor?'

'You didn't ask.'

'But—'

'No. You tell me about this "competition" first.'

She raised her glass in irritation. 'It's like Carmen said. The one who turns in the best profile gets the promotion. They picked two businessmen nobody had managed to interview in more than a decade, and they assigned us one each.'

'Are you sure she's such a threat? She doesn't look it.'

'Don't be taken in by Carmen's appearance. She's got an MBA from Harvard and a cold barracuda mind to go with those curves. She's out to win. And, given the way Drago seems so accommodating, she's already got his full co-operation.'

'It looks like she's got one hell of a lot more than that.'

She looked up at him, remembering the way his lips had lingered over Carmen's fingers and how he'd taken his own good time releasing her. 'That could have been you, you know.'

He blinked into the pause. 'You mean you would have profiled Drago and I would have enjoyed the company of the vivacious Carmen?'

She did her best to ignore the 'enjoyed' part of his comment. 'It might have been easier for everyone. It certainly would have been easier for me.'

'You're forgetting something. You know why I agreed to this profile. You blackmailed me—remember? Said you'd go public on what happened eight years ago if I didn't go along with you. I doubt if even the very come-hither Carmen could have come up with something as creative as that.'

Saskia shrugged. 'Given the way Carmen fills that silver gown, she probably wouldn't have needed to. Creativity would have been the last thing on your mind.'

This time he smiled, lifting a hand and catching one looping tendril, winding it around his fingers, letting it slip through, winding it again. Her scalp tingled from the contact.

That much made sense—but why was it her breasts were suddenly straining, her nipples peaking? And why could she feel heat pooling inside, way down deep?

'I take your point,' he acknowledged, his voice unexpectedly husky, his eyes dark like a moonless night sky, the reflection from the chandeliers like the stars. 'But would you really rather I had Carmen? That wouldn't bother you?'

She swallowed as his face dipped lower, his eyes intent on her mouth. On her lips. And he could be doing this with Carmen? Oh, yes, it would bother her!

Was that what he was trying to prove right now?

'Of course not,' she lied, twisting away so that she tugged her hair from his fingers, carefully ensuring she avoided his eyes at the same time. What did he think—that she was jealous? Not a chance! She leaned her arms on the railing, looking out over the sea of brilliantly dressed guests in the ballroom below.

'If you say so,' he said. 'Although I for one am very pleased you ended up with me.'

Her heart did a slow roll and she turned her face up to meet his again. 'And why is that?'

'Because you'd be wasted on Drago. I didn't save your virginity for the likes of him.'

Shock rooted her to the spot as white-hot fury infused her veins, and only the fact they were in one of the top function rooms in the world, surrounded by the cream of society, stopped her from flinging the contents of her glass in his face.

'How dare you? I can't believe you just said that.'

'Why? You'd rather throw it away on someone like him?'

'How dare you pretend that you somehow "saved" me by what you did, and that that gives you the right to decide whom I make love to. It has nothing to do with you.'

Alex whirled around, pinning her between his body and the balustrade, his face close to her own. 'Now, that's where you're wrong. It has *everything* to do with me. I could have taken all you offered that night, I could have pushed my way into you. I could have deflowered you and used you and discarded you when I'd had enough. But I didn't. I let you go. But not so you could throw it away on some lecherous businessman old enough to be your grandfather.'

'Who says I would have thrown it away on him?'

'It doesn't matter. Whether you threw it or whether he demanded it as payment for his profile, it amounts to the same thing. A total waste.'

Her chest heaving, her temperature off the wall, and her body reacting to his coarse words as if she'd been shot with hormones, she spun around in his arms until she could rest against the balustrade and not be forced to look into those deep, dark eyes. 'I can't believe we're having this conversation.'

But turning around proved a big mistake. He moved closer behind her, so she could feel his warm breath on her ear, feel his body press full length against hers, wedging her tight against the balustrade. She gasped. He was aroused, and his hand snared her waist, dragging her even closer into contact with him, the sensation even through layers of fabric still shockingly intimate, irresistibly carnal.

'So tell me,' he urged, his voice low and thick in her ear, 'what would you rather be doing?'

Every part of her wanted to lean back into his heated strength. Even now her back ached to arch, ached to send that low part of her in motion against him, ached to feel his length caress her. What was he doing to her? Turning her wanton and reckless at the first hint of sex?

Purposefully she fought the battle going on inside her,

battled to quell the swelling of her breasts and nipples and secret places. Battled to suppress the need.

'I want…' she whispered.

'Yes?' he murmured, the tip of his tongue tracing the line of her ear.

'To get this profile done and go home.'

He stilled, and she could feel the disbelief blow holes in his sexual energy. 'The profile?'

'That's why I'm here, after all. Nothing more.'

He let go his hold on her and she slipped out of his reach, covering her relief at her escape by smoothing her skirts.

'So how important is it, this competition? Do you want to win?'

'Of course I want to win!' *I have to win.* 'Why else do you think I bothered to track you down? It certainly wasn't to chew over the fat and talk about old times.'

Why else indeed? He looked intently at her. She must really need this promotion desperately to go to the trouble she had, to risk another encounter with him. And, dammit, why had she walked back into his life? He didn't need reminders of the past. He didn't need the risk to his present. So why the hell couldn't he just leave her alone? 'What's so important?'

Saskia looked back over the crowd below—couples moving on the jam-packed dance floor, small groups gathered around the fringe, talking and laughing. 'What do you care? Isn't it enough that I want this promotion?'

'No, it's not enough.' He was angry now. Angry at all the old emotions she'd brought up. Angry that he couldn't forget them. 'What would make you desperate enough to come looking for me after what happened between us? You must have known the sparks would·fly. So what is it that you want—the honour, the prestige?'

She shook her head as she leaned out over the highly polished brass railing. 'No, it's not the prestige.'

'Then it must be money. How much do you need? I can give you money.'

The words were out before he even realised, before he even knew that he meant them. But money was something he could do. Easily. He had more than enough for himself, and if it meant getting rid of her any faster then it would be money well spent.

She looked up at him, her green eyes filled with disbelief. 'You'd do that? You'd give me money?'

Hell, yes, if it meant getting her out of his hair and his life back to normal.

'How much do you need?'

She shook her head.

'I don't want your money. I'm expecting to win this competition. All I need is your co-operation so I can make this profile the best it can be.'

'And if you don't win?'

'I'm going to win.'

'Don't be so stubborn. If it's money you need, I can give it to you.'

'And why would you do that? Why would you suddenly want to give money to the woman you've accused of being the lowest of the low, somebody stalking your sister to get the goods to plaster all over the nearest gossip rag?'

'What was I expected to think, finding you sneaking around taking photographs outside my home at the same time the paparazzi were clamouring for Marla's blood?' He swiped a hand back through his hair. Damn! He was supposed to be trying to convince her to take the money and go, not rehash every problem they already had. 'Look, why not let me help you? Consider it compensation for past transgressions, if you like.'

Her face moved beyond shock to anger in an instant, her green eyes vivid, narrowed in accusation.

'You want to give me *money* because you threw me out of your bed before smashing apart my father's existence? What are you looking for—absolution? Do you think you can pay me off for what you did? That money somehow makes it better? You don't even know how much I need. One hundred thousand dollars? Five hundred? How about one million? How much are you prepared to fork out to assuage your guilt?'

'That's enough!'

'No amount would be enough!' she remonstrated, thankful for the cover of music but still trying to keep her voice low. 'I was seventeen years old, bowled over by the attentions of the best-looking man I'd ever seen. He made me feel like a princess. For weeks he treated me like his queen—and it was all such an outright lie. In one awful night he smashed my hopes and dreams. The next day he smashed my father's. He made a fool out of us both. *Totally humiliated us both.* And now he thinks he can pay me off for what he did with cold, hard cash? Not a chance.'

'Your father deserved everything he got!'

'So you say. Because he ruined your own family's business more than twenty years before. What a nerve! But you sure made him pay for that. What I don't understand is what I did to deserve it too.'

He looked away, his teeth clenched, blood pounding in his head, feeling his hatred for her father pulse through him like a living thing. Feeling hatred for the man he'd been becoming loom up like a gigantic shadow over his life. But what could he say? She was right. She'd done nothing to deserve it.

'It could have been worse,' he bit out at last.

'You think? How the hell could it have been any worse?'

'I could have finished off what I started. I could have made love to you that night after all.'

CHAPTER SEVEN

A THUNDERBOLT of silence followed his remark. Finally she could speak. 'You're right,' Saskia said, but all the while her heart was screaming, *Liar*. 'Thank God I was spared that.'

The look in his eyes, shuttered and bleak, was satisfaction indeed. He glanced down at his watch.

'There are speeches coming up. And then we're leaving,' he announced.

'Already? And just when we're having so much fun.'

Scowling, Alex escorted her down the stairs, Saskia heading for the refuge of the ladies' lounge while he sought out the event's organisers.

The lounge was like a sanctuary inside, the velvet wallpaper, luxurious drapes and deep tub chairs making the room feel more like a sitting room than a bathroom.

She stood at the basins, holding a damp cloth to her heated face. What was it about that man? Lulling her into a false sense of security one minute, digging deep under her skin the next?

The door behind her swung open and she caught the flash of silver satin in the mirror. Saskia let her eyes fall shut and suppressed a groan. The last person she really wanted to see right now was Carmen. Her sanctuary had suddenly turned to hell.

'Things getting a little heated between you two lovers then?' she enquired.

'I've just got something in my eye,' Saskia responded, dabbing the cloth under her lowered eyelashes, uncomfortable with the thought that Carmen had been watching them. She pulled the fabric away, glancing down at the cloth. 'There,' she said smiling, *pretending*, before screwing it into a ball and tossing it into the waste. She turned around as if she was about to leave. 'Are you enjoying the ball? Alex said the speeches are about to begin. I must join him.'

'You're not going to win, you know. This job is going to be mine.' Carmen's face was set into a mask so tightly bound with loathing that Saskia felt the first stirrings of fear. They'd never been what she'd call friends, but this naked anger was something new. Something frightening.

'You seem pretty sure of yourself,' Saskia replied calmly, trying to avoid a slanging match and wishing Carmen would move away from the door so she could escape. 'Good luck with your profile, in that case.'

'So how did you do it?' Carmen asked, not moving an inch.

'How did I do what, exactly?'

'Get Alex to agree to marry you. I thought he'd be the last guy you'd want to get hooked up with after the way he wiped your father's company off the face of the earth.'

Saskia did a double take. 'You know about that? How the hell—?'

Carmen smiled—if you could call the way her lips thinned and curved nastily a smile. 'I do thorough research. It's a particular skill of mine. Or one of them.' She tilted her head, her eyes glinting dangerously even in the subdued lighting. 'Did you think I'd leave it to chance who we were assigned to profile? Who do you think suggested the subjects?'

Saskia laughed. 'You can't be serious. The board would hardly let *you* choose them.'

'Oh, it wasn't that hard,' she boasted, feigning interest in her long scarlet nails. 'A word in an ear here, a hint in another ear there. Pretty soon they get together to discuss things, and *voila!* They're all in agreement. Suddenly it's all their idea. Only you want to ruin it all. You weren't supposed to like the guy, let alone marry him.'

She smiled again, and Saskia imagined it must be how a shark looked before it headed in for the kill.

'But now that too is working in my favour. Already the board is thinking you're not such a good prospect, given you'll be doing the maternity thing before too long. If, indeed, you're not already…'

She let her eyes settle on Saskia's abdomen like an accusation, leaving her words to hang there, letting them drip their poisoned content down slowly.

'Is there already a bastard child of Alexander Koutoufides festering inside you?'

Saskia prayed for strength. Because if she didn't she might just slap the other woman right here, right now. 'Don't you think that's a little unlikely? We've been together barely a week, after all.'

'Enough time to become engaged, however. Tell me, what's he like in bed? Drago is enthusiastic, if nothing else, but he lacks a certain—*finesse*. I'll wager that Alex lacks nothing.'

'Who says I've slept with him?'

'Come on—you're getting married. No man in Alex's position would agree to such a thing without testing the merchandise.'

'And if I told you there was no engagement? That there will be no marriage?'

'Then I'd think you were clutching at straws. And that you were so very, very sad. Because that would mean you'll soon be without a job *and* a man.' She sighed theatrically. 'In that case, enjoy him now, while you can.'

Saskia reefed in a deep breath, trying to quell the mounting sickness inside her. 'You must want this job awfully desperately if you're prepared to lie and cheat to get it.'

'Oh, yes,' Carmen agreed brightly, not even making a pretence at disagreeing with Saskia's summing up. 'And I'm going to get it too.'

Saskia had heard enough. She gathered up her skirts in both hands and drove a straight line for the door, forcing Carmen to back off at the last moment as she soared past, leaving her parting words in her wake.

'Just don't count on it.'

'You missed the speeches.'

Alex slipped her wrap around her shoulders and she grunted her thanks. If he thought she must still be angry from their argument he didn't say anything, and she was glad he didn't pursue it. She was too tightly wound from her run-in with Carmen to make sense right now.

From across the foyer Drago waved and caught her eye, gesturing as if he wanted to talk. Alex steered her purposefully towards the door regardless. 'Come on,' he said.

'Drago—' she said, gesturing to her right in case he hadn't seen.

'I saw him,' he replied, and just kept going, directing her towards the doorman and a line of waiting limousines. The doorman pulled open the rear passenger door for them and waited for her to gather her skirts and climb in.

'Why do I get the impression you're not too fond of Drago?'

'Who says I'm not?' he rejoined, following her in, all lean grace and fluid movement.

The car drove away, and something about the way he'd answered piqued her interest.

'And yet you obviously have so much in common. Both of you hold status as business success stories who prefer to live life out of the public eye. And both of you share the Baxter Foundation in common.'

His jaw twitched markedly as he settled alongside her. 'Hasn't it occurred to you yet? Some people stay out of the public eye because they're naturally private people. Others simply can't stand up to public scrutiny.'

The meaning behind his words was more than clear. 'You're suggesting Drago is into something shady?'

Dark eyes collided with hers. 'I've done business with him in the past. And on the basis of that experience I would never choose to do business with him again.'

'Surely you're not suggesting there's anything underhand about Drago's business interests?'

The look he gave her was intentionally non-committal. 'Just be glad you're not the one doing his profile.'

He settled back into his seat, very relieved again that it wasn't Saskia who'd drawn the Drago Maiolo assignment. Just the thought of those squat diamond-encrusted and nicotine stained fingers anywhere near the sweet curves of Saskia thickened his breathing to growling point. She was still a virgin. Much too good for the likes of Drago.

Hell, she was far too good for anyone. And, no matter who her father was or what he had done, after the way Alex had treated her once before, he included himself in that number.

But that didn't make him stop wanting her.

She'd fitted into his arms tonight as if she was made for

him, her head tucked under his chin, her body pressed within a heartbeat of his, and no longer was she the teenage goddess-in-waiting who had been so hard to walk away from back then. Now she was the real deal, her body rich with the power of her femininity, ripe and lush. *Ready.*

Even now her scent worked its way across the space between them, calling out to him, tempting him. Even now the jade-green colour of her eyes was the colour he saw when he closed his own eyes. Even now, separated by several feet of the finest leather upholstery...

Damn it!

Even now she was making him hard!

'So which one are you?' she asked softly from across the car, cutting into his thoughts.

He turned away from the window and the unseen passing parade of Manhattan buildings. 'What do you mean?'

'Are you merely a naturally private person?' she continued. 'Or is there something you're trying to hide?'

He looked across at her. 'What do you think?' he challenged.

She looked at him for a moment, her features still, her eyes assessing, her lips slightly parted. 'I know you weren't always so media-shy. Something must have happened that made you go low-profile.'

He didn't like the direction this conversation was taking. She wouldn't like it if he went there. 'You're forgetting about Marla. Don't you think one headliner in any family is enough?'

She stared at him. 'Maybe,' she said, as if she'd already written off that possibility. 'Or maybe there's something else you're trying to hide. Why did you drop off the face of the earth like you did?'

Moments expanded into seconds. Seconds expanded into for ever. And a muscle in his jaw worked through it all. Should he tell her that it all went back to that night? That he'd seen what he was becoming, what he was turning into, and he'd run the other way?

Then the car pulled into the drive-through at their hotel, her door was pulled open, a bubble of sounds and light invaded their uncomfortable silence, and the moment was gone.

'I'll co-operate with you on the profile,' he said at last as they exited the car. 'And I'll give you all the time you need to give you the best chance of winning. But there's something I need in return.'

'What is it?' she asked, almost too enthusiastically. If Carmen was going to undermine her every attempt to win this job she was going to need Alex's full co-operation. That would be worth almost anything.

'I want your guarantee that you'll leave Marla out of it. I don't want you having anything to do with her and I don't want her mentioned. Understand?'

She was about to agree unreservedly before she remembered the notebook she had stashed in her luggage—the notebook she'd promised to read. It was a promise she'd made to the woman that she wasn't about to break, no matter what Alex demanded. Besides, it wasn't as if she was about to include anything from it in her profile. Alex might doubt it, but her sense of ethics went a little deeper than that. 'This has always been about you, not Marla. I intend leaving her right out of the profile.'

His eyes drilled into her, as if he were digging into her very soul for the truth.

'Just keep it that way,' was all he said.

It was only when she was alone in her plush suite and getting ready for bed that she realised he'd never answered her

question. Why was that? What *had* provoked Alex
Koutoufides's sudden departure from public view? What was
he trying to hide, and why?

Saskia shrugged as she rehung tonight's gorgeous gown.
Did it matter? At least she'd secured his co-operation.
Tomorrow she could really start work. She'd assemble the ad-
ditional reports she needed, she'd have her questions ready,
and by the sounds of it he might even let her into the house
to watch him at work in his study, managing his empire from
half a world away.

Until then she had another job to do. She pulled the fluffy
white hotel robe around her and flopped onto the wide bed,
propping a pillow under her chest and picking up the red
notebook. Her reviewing it obviously meant so much to
Marla, but she really wasn't relishing the prospect. Even with
a celebrity name behind it, the writing would still have to
stand on its own merits, and the chance of publication was a
long shot. Hopefully Marla understood that.

Reluctantly she contemplated the cover, where Marla had
penned the working title *From the Inside*, expecting to be
able to offer nothing more than an honest yet encouraging
critique—something she hoped wouldn't crush the woman's
hopes and dreams in the process. It was obvious she needed
something in her life to make her feel worthwhile. Maybe
writing was it.

Saskia turned the cover and started to read.

About a young girl finding her place in the world—a young
girl whose perfect, cherished life changed when she encoun-
tered sex at the age of fifteen, at the hands of a much older
man, a young girl who discovered how much she enjoyed the
act and yearned to learn more, who *set out* to learn more.

It told the story of the impact when her parents died in a

horrific boating fire at sea, and how she'd lurched into her marriages. It relived the short-lived bliss and the disasters they'd became. It told of her endless flirtation with celebrity. It covered everything: her slide into drug and alcohol dependency, her time behind the walls drying out, having therapy, thinking she was sane, knowing she must be mad.

It told of a woman who needed to heal herself. A woman who had recognised that it was time to grow up.

The prose wasn't perfect. It was raw, and needed editing and organisation, but the account pulled no punches. It was brutally honest, and it didn't make the author out to be anything more than what she was, but it was funny and gritty and poignant at the same time, and touching beyond belief.

Hours after she'd started, and with tears in her eyes, Saskia closed the notebook. Marla was a remarkable woman. She'd claimed she had no talents, but the woman who'd written this was gifted and insightful and deserved to be given the chance to succeed. If Saskia could do anything to help her, she would. And while she was in New York she had the perfect opportunity—she knew just the person. A former colleague from her magazine now worked in editorial for a publishing house, and lived not far from here. She'd be doing her a favour and getting Marla a second opinion.

In a fizz of excitement she'd reached for the phone at her bedside before she noticed the time. It wasn't long till dawn. She snuggled into bed and snapped off the light, feeling better than she'd felt in ages. She'd call after she'd snatched a few hours' sleep.

Alex was pounding on her door when she raced out of the lift shortly before noon.

'I'm here,' Saskia said breathlessly.

'Where the hell have you been?' he demanded, as she used her room key to unlock the door and pushed it open. 'I've been calling for ages.'

'Nowhere special. I just…went out for a walk.'

'Our car will be here in ten minutes.' His words trailed her into the room.

'It's okay. I'm just about packed.' She didn't bother to take off her jacket even though she felt as if she was burning up after running back. Instead she just threw her purse on a chair and grabbed the last of her toiletries from the bathroom. She zipped them into a bag and turned straight into a wall. The wall of his chest. His hands went to her shoulders, anchoring her before she could step away.

'What's the rush?'

'You said the car—'

'There's time.' He touched a hand to her chin, lifting it so her eyes had no choice but to collide with his. 'Your face is pink.'

She knew full well that her colour couldn't only be attributed to her race to get back. A large dollop of it was relief at completing her task this morning. Her former colleague had been as keen to see Marla's story as she'd expected. Her excitement at reading the first chapter had mirrored Saskia's own, and right now she couldn't wait to get back to Tahoe and let Marla know an editor was considering her work.

As for the rest of her colour? It was due entirely to the way he was making her feel right now, pressed so close to her, his fingers adding an electric thrum to her overheated skin. 'I ran,' she said, when she'd located the thin thread of her voice at last. 'A few blocks. That's all.'

'Maybe you should calm down a little.'

His voice had a husky quality that didn't fit with a rush to the car. Where was his urgency? Where was the panic she'd seen when she'd found him pounding on her door?

She laughed, a half-hearted attempt that sounded as pitiable as it felt. How the hell was she supposed to calm down with him standing over her—touching her?

'Thanks. I will. Now…if you'll excuse me…I'll finish my packing.'

This time he let her go, standing in the doorway, one arm behind his neck, as she stashed the toiletries bag and locked down her luggage.

'I'm ready,' she said, her senses reeling once more from experiencing the let-down after a close encounter with Alex: the sensual build-up, the pull of his body on hers, only to be let go, to be spun out like wreckage from a hurricane, thrown out to crash wherever it landed. It was crazy. How could he have this effect on her when she didn't want anything to do with him?

He pushed himself away from the door to follow her. 'Before we go,' he started, 'last night I offered you money. You objected then, but maybe overnight you thought about it. Maybe you reconsidered. I want you to know my offer is still open.'

She closed her eyes for a second, breathing in deep. She'd said too much last night, way too much. She'd reacted too violently to his offer of money and she'd made it sound as if her pain was still raw, that it still mattered.

But it didn't matter any more! She was over it. And if it wasn't for Alex, scraping back the intervening years, peeling back time as if he was ripping off a thick scab and revealing the wound, raw and stinging and deep, the past would have stayed safely where she'd buried it.

'No,' she said at last, slinging the strap of her purse over her shoulder. 'You should never have offered me money.

Especially not for the reason you did. But let's not talk about it any more. It's in the past. Let it stay there.'

He took a step closer, bridging the gap between them. 'Saskia, think about it. You could forget all about this bizarre contest.' He reached out a hand to her arm. 'You could leave now.'

She reeled back. 'Don't touch me!'

A muscle twitched in his cheek, his eyes turned hard as steel. 'You'll never forgive me for what happened, will you?'

'Why should I?' she insisted. 'You can't buy me off. It simply should never have happened in the first place.'

His dark eyes glinted, his jaw square. 'I had my reasons.'

'What? Now you're telling me you had *reasons*? You really have a nerve. I have no idea what kind of sick reasons you think would excuse the way you acted, and I really don't want to know.'

'No,' he muttered, trying to control his anger-coated breathing as she marched out of the room ahead of him. 'I don't imagine you do.'

Marla must have been anxious for news. She was already waiting for her early the next morning, when Saskia took a walk along the lake's edge. Her jeans and thick sweater were keeping out the early-morning chill, although she was already regretting not tying her hair back against the breeze that whipped her curls around her face and turned them to stinging tendrils.

'How was the ball?' Marla asked, a nervous excitement in her smile.

Saskia nodded. 'It was entertaining in places.'

'Good,' she said brightly, and Saskia could see that for all her anxiousness she was too afraid to ask.

'Marla, about that writing…'

'Yes?'

'I know it was yours.'

The older woman looked contrite and laced an arm through Saskia's as they walked out onto the pier. 'Oh, I'm sorry. I thought you might say no if you knew it was mine. And I did so want your opinion on it.' She looked up at Saskia, hope in her eyes. 'So…did you get a chance to read it? What did you think?'

Saskia smiled. The older woman's enthusiasm was infectious. 'Well, first of all, you know how hard it is to get work published, don't you? Some people struggle for years and years and never make it.'

Marla's face dropped. 'Are you saying it was no good, then?'

'No. I thought it was very good.'

'Really? You really did?'

She laughed. 'I really did.'

Still with their arms entwined, Marla clapped her gloved hands together and jumped up and down. 'That's fantastic. So where's the problem?'

'I just don't want you to get your hopes up too high. I've left the book with an editor friend of mine in New York. She was very interested, but it still doesn't mean—'

'You've got an editor reading it? My book?' Marla pulled her arms free and slapped both hands over her mouth. 'That's so fantastic. Oh, Saskia, thank you so, so much!'

She threw her arms around the younger woman and hugged her tight.

'It's great news,' Saskia agreed. 'But don't be too disappointed if they can't use it—okay? There are plenty more publishers out there after all. I'm sure there's one for you somewhere—it might just take a while.'

'Oh, my, I just can't believe it,' Marla said, giving Saskia another squeeze. 'I'm so glad you came. This is the best news I've ever had.'

They walked along the shore, talking companionably, Marla pumping her for comments on various parts of her story, and all the while the wind was picking up. Getting more frustrated with herself for not tying it back, Saskia pushed her hair off her face one more time. 'This hair is driving me crazy.'

Marla looked up at her. 'I love your hair. Those curls make it look so alive, and I just love the colour.' She pulled back the hood of her jacket and ran a hand over her own silvery blonde mane. 'Do you think that colour would suit me? I think it's time I had a change.'

Saskia smiled, recognising immediately that the warmer colour would suit Marla's skin tones perfectly. 'I think it would look great.'

'You wouldn't mind if I tried?'

'Why should I mind? I think you'd look sensational.'

They talked for a while together, about hairstyles and colours, and families, getting to know more about each other, building an easy camaraderie. Until a voice called out through the pines.

'Marla!'

She spun around. 'Oh, God, I've been too long. That's Jake, looking for me. That guy is driving me totally crazy, you know. I'd better run.' She kissed Saskia quickly on the cheek, gave more hurried thanks, and headed off quickly for the house.

Finally Saskia had a chance to get some much needed work done. Alex had been true to his word and had invited her into his large state-of-the-art office, complete with computers, fax and even teleconferencing facilities. 'Wow,' she said, contemplating the screen and taking some shots with the digital camera he'd finally conceded she might need to do her job. 'What a set-up. You've got everything you need to do business anywhere in the world right here.'

'That's the idea. Now that my portfolio is spread so widely, I can't be in every place at once. This is the next best thing.'

He pulled some files out of an oak filing cabinet while she looked at the photographs on his desk. There was one very old one of his family alongside a fishing boat. She picked it up and smiled. Alex must have been around ten or so, his arms crossed and his stance wide, as if he was the boss, but his smile was cheeky as he looked into the camera. Marla stood alongside, looking like a young colt, not that much taller for her years, but all long legs, unbridled energy and classic beauty, even though she must have been just a young teenager. His parents stood behind, his olive-skinned father with an arm around his fair mother's shoulders. Marla's story mentioned they'd died in a boating accident. Had it been that same boat they'd died on?

'My parents,' Alex said softly, pulling the photo from her hands and placing it back on his wide desk.

'How old were you when they died?'

He sighed, at the same time dropping a stack of glossy reports and financial statements on the desk before turning to look out through the large windows into the distance. 'Fourteen.'

'That's so not fair. My mother died when I was still too little to remember her. I can't imagine what it would have been like to have lost her as a teenager.'

He looked over his shoulder at her. 'What happened to her?'

'Breast cancer, apparently. She was too scared to see the doctors, and by the time she did it was too late. But I was a baby, so I don't have any memories of her at all. I think in some ways that's easier. I can't imagine losing both of my parents in such a horrific accident, though. That must have been devastating.'

He turned around completely, his brows drawn together. 'You know how my parents died? How is that? I don't remember telling you.'

She swallowed, suddenly guilty because it had been Marla's memoirs that had filled in the details for her. 'I must have read it somewhere. In my background notes, maybe.'

He considered her answer for a while, his eyes holding hers, locked in the past, swirling with pain. 'Sometimes I think they really died after the takeover. It broke them, you know.' Then he seemed to snap back to the present. He grunted and sat down opposite her. 'If you want this profile, we should get started. Here's what I've got for you to look at already…'

They were still in his office hours later, when the call came through. The late afternoon sun slanted through the long windows and a fresh breeze stirred the curtains, making one think of closing up windows and doors—that the best part of the day would soon be over.

Alex listened for a moment before handing the receiver over. 'It's for you, from London,' he said. 'A Rodney Krieg?'

She accepted the phone while Alex pushed back in his chair, his arms behind his head, his feet crossed on the desk. 'Sir Rodney? I didn't expect to hear from you so soon.'

'Saskia, my dear.' Sir Rodney's gruff voice churned down the line. 'How are you getting on over there?'

'Great. The profile's going really well.' She nodded at Alex. 'I've got Alex's full co-operation—I should be finished within the week.'

'Ah…' blustered the voice at the other end. 'About that profile…'

A cold shiver of trepidation shimmied its way down her

spine. 'What about it?' she asked, her voice tight with concern. 'Is there a problem?'

Alex leaned forward in his chair and she swivelled her own away, so she didn't have to look at him. She didn't need him in on this conversation.

'Well, it's just that the board's more than a little concerned…'

Trepidation gave way to dread.

'About what?'

'There's some talk that you might be going to withdraw from the contest.'

'Why would I do that? I've been working towards this job for at least the last twelve months. Why would I suddenly give it all up?'

'You might if you were worried about taking on such a demanding role in London when you're thinking about settling down and starting a family somewhere else. This is a demanding role. It's no place for a part-time employee or commuter. I expect you realise that. Now in this day and age we can hardly discriminate against you on such grounds—that wouldn't be right at all, of course. But we can ask if you seriously want to proceed to with this application or not—and if not, then it might be wiser to withdraw.'

Her heart skipped a beat. She couldn't be hearing this.

'No, no, Sir Rodney. I explained all that. There is not going to be any marriage. This engagement isn't real. It's just for show—just a diversion for the press to get the focus off Marla. Obviously it must be working, or the board wouldn't be thinking it's real.'

'Now, now,' he soothed, with no conviction at all. 'I know that's what you told me. But you're forgetting one thing. Carmen saw you together at that Baxter Foundation night, looking very much the part, and now the papers are reporting

Alex as saying you're going to be married as soon as possible. There's even some talk that a family might not be too far distant.'

Saskia's blood froze. There was no mistaking where those whispers would have come from. 'Did that come from Carmen? Because she's told me she'll do anything to win that promotion. Can't you see what she's doing?'

'Does it really matter where it came from when it only serves to verify what the board already suspects?'

'Of course it matters! Please believe me, Sir Rodney, there will be no wedding! I told you, it's not a real engagement.'

'I'm sorry, Saskia.' Sir Rodney was sounding impatient. 'I know how much this promotion means to you, and I know how hard you've worked, but the board is having trouble accepting that this engagement to a man like Alex Koutoufides can be anything but real—it doesn't make sense. They don't want to find out after they've made a decision that you've decided you're no longer available for the job. This role is too important.'

'But I wouldn't!'

'Besides which, Carmen has already handed in a preliminary report. It's excellent—just what we're after. Frankly, the board are wondering if there's any point proceeding with the contest.'

'But Sir Rodney…'

There was a moment's hesitation. 'I'm sorry, Saskia. It might be for the best if you get notice of your withdrawal into the board sooner rather than later.'

Saskia held the phone to her ear even after the final click had signalled he was gone. Because even just holding it felt as if she wasn't giving up on her dream. Once she put down that phone it would be like acknowledging her chances were dead. And they couldn't be dead.

She'd done everything she could possibly do for this job—

she'd agreed to profile the person she detested more than anyone in the world, the person who'd destroyed her family and whom she held responsible for setting her father on his decline to despair and illness. She hadn't wanted to profile Alex, but she'd agreed because it was the only way that would ensure she had the means of providing the kind of care her father needed and deserved. That or she'd drag him down in the process.

She'd done everything she possibly could, and it was still not enough. Once again her hopes and dreams had been thwarted.

And it was all down to one man.

The man sitting opposite her right now.

Alexander Koutoufides!

She took a deep breath and turned her chair back round, replacing the long-dead receiver, finally acknowledging what she'd known all along—there was no lifeline. No lifeline, no white knight to ride out on a charger and save her, no fairies at the bottom of the garden. This was real life, and if she needed saving she was going to have to do it herself.

'What's wrong?' he asked from across the desk. 'What's happened?'

She lifted her eyes to meet his, momentarily taken aback at the level of concern she saw there—but only momentarily. He didn't mean it. He didn't care about her or her job, and least of all her father. He'd used her once again and this was the result. Another disaster. Another nightmare. And all at the hands of Alex Koutoufides. Oh, Carmen Rivers might have taken advantage of the situation, but it had been manufactured by this one man.

She stood—unable to sit, unable to control the buzzing forces that screamed for release inside her, unable to control the trembling fury that possessed every muscle.

'You bastard!' she seethed. 'You total bastard. If you hadn't insisted on all this engagement garbage—if you hadn't told every reporter going that you couldn't wait to get married—'

'Hey,' he said coming around the desk towards her. 'What am I supposed to have done?'

'I'm out of the running for the promotion. The board has decided that it can't give me the position—regardless of the profile I turn in—because it wouldn't be fair to the magazine or to *our marriage*.'

'I thought you'd already explained what was going on.'

'I had! And I thought he finally believed me. But you had to insist on taking me to New York. You insisted on me wearing a fortune in your mother's diamonds to flash in front of everyone, including the one person I was competing with for the position. And then you had to tell the press that we were getting married as soon as possible. Now there's no chance I can get that job. It doesn't matter what I do, or how this profile turns out, they won't give it to me. And it's all your fault!'

'But they can't do that, surely? Whether or not you're married is irrelevant. They can't discriminate against you on those grounds.'

'They're not! They're expecting me to withdraw. Especially now Carmen has already given them a teaser of *her* profile. They're not even interested in anything I might present.'

Her chest heaving, her breathing ragged, she battled to control her thoughts. There had to be an answer. There just had to be.

He rounded the desk towards her and she spun away as he spoke. 'Maybe things aren't as bad as you think?'

'You have no idea how bad!' That job should have been hers. The chance to see her father was cared for decently—it had been within her grasp. She'd fought so hard for it. She'd more than paid the price. Only to have success snatched cruelly and bitterly from her. 'You have no idea what you've done or what you've cost me. You ruined my life eight years ago and you've ruined it all over again. You couldn't have ruined it more thoroughly if you'd tried.'

She felt a hand on her shoulder and spun back round, lashing out with her hands, wanting to beat her fists against his chest, wanting to strike him and pound him and hurt him so that he'd know something of what she was feeling. Something of the pain. Something of the despair.

'I hate you Alex Koutoufides. I hate you to hell and back!'

She couldn't see him, but still she struck out. Tears distorted her vision and anguish distorted her mind, but still she pounded away. Only the pain was focused, sharp and deep and burning hot. And the pain tore through everything, savagely slicing open old wounds, jaggedly ripping through her heart, fuelling her beating muscles, screaming out the truth.

She'd failed.

She'd been so close to succeeding, so close to success that she'd been able to taste it, and yet still she'd failed. Now she would have nothing to offer her father. Now there would be nothing she could do for him. Nothing.

There was no point any more. There was no reason to fight any more. Everything she'd battled for, everything she'd held precious, was worth nothing. And now she had nothing left to lose. There was nothing left to fight for.

She was like a hurricane in his arms, unpredictable, unstoppable, a powerhouse of energy and emotion that had to spin itself out. All he could do was hold her, let herself work it out of her system and take it out on him.

Except he couldn't wait.

She was in his arms, passionate, desperate, and he was passionate and desperate enough to take advantage of it. How could he resist the erratic pounding of her heart, the frantic rise and fall of her breasts, her scent, and the sweet press of her feminine curves so close to his own? Why should he even bother?

He dropped his head, pressed his mouth to the top of her head, burying his lips in her mussed hair, inhaling the warm scent of woman—this one special woman.

Her breathing caught and she stilled her fight momentarily, giving him a chance to reach a hand under her chin and turn her face up to meet his. Her eyes were cloudy and damp, but warm, like the sky after a tropical storm, her lips moist and pink and slightly parted.

He shook his head. What the hell was he thinking? But then, what did it matter anyway? These thoughts skipped through his brain before he decided that thinking was surplus to requirements and dipped his mouth to hers because it seemed like the most natural thing in the world.

The most obvious thing.

The most inevitable thing.

Her breath caught and she froze, fought for an instant, and then relaxed as his mouth refused to let go of hers. She tasted of that storm and its aftermath, of maelstrom giving way to peace, of tempest followed by calm. And her lips moved under his. And as they did her body changed again, her breathing quickening, her energy returning, so that he could feel it as a living, pulsing force.

And soon the storm was back.

She was giving as good as she got, her lips demanding more, her tongue seeking his own. Her arms found purchase around his body and she pressed herself up against him, so close it was as if she wanted to be part of him, and he ached to make her so. Then she forced her hands up between their bodies, her nails raking against his shirt, unzipping his desire, before pulling his mouth down on hers again. Did she realise what she was doing to him? Did she have any idea what her body was inviting?

'Sto thiavolo,' he murmured against her ear, her answering shudder feeding into his wants and desires. To hell with it, indeed. The rush of blood through his veins told him he was going there for sure.

She wasn't asking him to stop, and somehow he knew he was no longer capable of it anyway.

'What are you doing?' she asked, her voice thick with need, as he swung her into his arms and carried her through a short passageway to a sprawling bedroom.

He pressed his lips to her forehead and let them linger, sampling her sweetness, tasting her desire. Then he drew back and lost himself in her green, green eyes.

'Something I should have done a long time ago.'

CHAPTER EIGHT

LIFE didn't come with second chances, let alone third. Alex knew that. All his life he'd taken his opportunities when and wherever they appeared and not relied on waiting for a second chance to come around. He'd clawed his way back from having nothing because of it. He'd built his success around it. And in the unlikely event that he'd missed an opportunity he'd lived with the consequences.

He'd had his chance with Saskia Prentice eight years ago. He'd had it and he'd blown it, and he had been happy to live with the consequences. Well, maybe not happy, but resigned. He knew the way he'd treated her back then had been a mistake, he knew what he'd lost before it had been gained, but then this was the price he'd had to pay.

But now life was giving him a second chance. And what with second chances coming around so rarely, no way was he going to mess this up.

It was like a gift from the gods. He laid her down on the bed, intending to shrug off his clothes before he joined her, but one look into her large green eyes and he knew that his place was there, alongside her, right now. He took the time to lever off no more than his shoes before he lowered himself, fully clothed, gathering her close. *'Agape mou,'* he told her, because right at this moment the English language didn't seem large enough to describe what he felt. 'You're so beautiful,' he said, echoing what his eyes had already told her. Then it was the turn of his lips and his hands to prove it.

The sun moved lower in the sky, the breeze carried more of a chill, but inside the room temperatures were soaring exponentially with need. He wanted to feel every part of her, to taste every part of her, all at once.

And she was hungry too—her hands reaching out for him, reefing out his shirt, seeking out his skin. And knowing she wanted him only ramped up his own need tenfold.

She was a virgin. He'd had the opportunity before to accept her gift eight years ago and he'd blown it. And yet here she was, still entrusting him with the heady responsibility of showing her the full magic of being a woman, and the supreme power of what she could do to a man.

And that was a gift indeed. A gift he wasn't about to turn away again. Not when he could have his fill of her and get her out of his system at the same time. Because if he had her he wouldn't crave her any more. It was worth making love to her simply for that.

His hands moved over her, hot and hungry, falling on her breasts, unpeeling clothes and lace and anything that got in the way of his need and his purpose. He cupped her breasts in his hands. He suckled her nipples, one after the other, feeling her body arch underneath him as she cried out in torturous pleasure, and she wrenched off his shirt, clamping him to her, demanding more.

He dispensed with his own jeans, then with her trousers, peeling them from her like a second skin, revealing the pearl-like skin of her long legs to his hungry gaze.

He ran his hands up their length as his kiss preceded them.

They were smooth legs, firm legs. Legs made to wrap around a man and draw him in close.

And right now he was that man.

His hands reached the top of her thighs, toying with the band of her silk panties, while her hands reached his head, her fingers raking through his hair, tugging, insistent.

'Alex,' she cried.

But he wasn't through with her yet. She hadn't felt all he could make her feel. He pressed his face against her and breathed in her rich feminine desire, a scent made just for him, just for this time. A scent that filled every remaining part of his mind and body with need.

He stripped away the underwear in an instant, parting her tenderly with his fingers, dipping his tongue and circling the lush pink bud within, dipping his tongue further and tasting her honeyed sweetness.

She cried out again, her hands clutching at his head, then pounding at her pillow as she bucked, then back again as he anchored her to her mouth, drawing out the sweetness, teasing out the pleasure.

'Please…' she pleaded.

He wanted to please her. He wanted to show her how good it could be. How good it *should* be. But it was so hard not to be waylaid by how perfect she was. He lifted his head and touched her gently with his fingers, feeling the liquid heat welcome him. He raised his eyes and watched her face as his fingers stroked her entrance and then entered her, first one and then another, feeling her tight silken heat envelop them, tugging, insistent, inviting, as his thumb continued to circle that tight bud.

'Alex!'

He wanted to take his time. He meant to. He knew she was

a virgin and he should go slowly. He knew he should take his time and make it as wonderful for her as he knew it was going to be for him. But the desperate edge to her voice, the keening note it contained, was his undoing.

Driven by need, compelled by desire, he moved between her thighs, spreading them wide, remembering only at the last instant to take precautions. He fumbled with the details. Any delay now was far too long. He'd waited eight long years as it was.

And then he was there. She held onto him, her arms entwined around his neck, her mouth working with his, welcoming his tongue inside as she would soon welcome him.

And he entered her, smoothly, cleanly, in one swift, painless thrust that took both her breath and her virginity away. And as she gripped him with new-found muscles that held him tight and dared him to go deeper, he heard in his heartbeat a distant echo of a former time. It made no sense, its rhythm drowned out by the force of what was happening between them, the power of his thrusts, the magic receptiveness of her body, tilting, angling to receive him even deeper. And deeper.

He was lost, her power taking him where it wanted, drawing him over the edge even as it took her. She stilled and came apart in his arms, her muscles contracting all around him like firecrackers until he had nowhere to go but to explode in the aftermath.

And it was only in the quietening minutes after that his heartbeat settled down once again into a steady rhythm that he could recognise. He listened to the beat, his limbs heavy in his post-sex state. He listened to what it told him. And it approved of his choice of bed partner. With her wild hair and lush curves and her too-wide mouth, she was a woman to hold onto, a woman you could love.

Theos! His body tensed, his spine chilled and his senses went from drowsy to red alert.

Where the hell had *that* come from? He couldn't love her. It would never happen. This was an exercise in taking what she'd offered, in getting her out of his system. Nothing more.

He shifted to one side, wanting suddenly to get away, yet strangely moved when she followed him, nestling in close. He looked at her, her eyes closed, her hair spread on the pillow like some coiled mantilla, a spiral curl of it falling over her cheek. Unable to resist, he lifted a hand, smoothing it back from her face, and her eyelids fluttered open.

Green eyes greeted him, moisture laden green eyes, and an unexpected guilt bit deep.

'Did I hurt you?'

Suddenly he realised that it mattered. That he didn't want to make her cry. And that made him even more unsettled.

'No,' she said. 'Were you supposed to?'

'I'm glad,' he said, more brusquely than he'd needed, avoiding the issue altogether. He didn't want to know why she was crying. He didn't want to muddy the waters any more when he didn't understand why sex should suddenly felt like something else entirely. But he wouldn't have to think about it for long—not if he could get her out of here quickly.

'I'm taking you to England tomorrow,' he said, his hand unable to resist sweeping gently along the dips and curves of her body even while planning his escape route

'England?' It was hard to think with him doing that, stirring her flesh all over again. Saskia had thought it couldn't be any better than that first time, but the way he had her feeling already made her think otherwise. But a trip to England? If they were anywhere near London she might have a chance to visit her father. 'Do you have business there?'

'No. We both do. I'm taking you to see Sir Rodney and the

board. I'm going to tell them the truth. I'm going to make them believe there never was an engagement.'

Something inside her chilled and set.

'You'd do that for me?' she asked. It was more than she'd ever expected from him, and yet still it was hard to sound excited about it.

'That promotion means so much to you. And it's because of me that you run the risk of losing it. It's the only thing I can do.'

It's not the only thing you can do, she wanted to argue. You could… What? What did she expect him to do? Admit his undying love for her? Marry her? On the strength of one hasty if spectacular sexual encounter? She didn't want that herself.

Did she?

But, no, she was no naïve teenager any more—and now she was no naïve virgin. She'd shed a tear as she'd waved one part of her life behind, even as she'd embraced the new. Because how could she feel the same and yet feel so different at the same time?

Right now it was too hard to think—much too hard to think. Especially when his mouth was weaving its magic on her skin and his hands were moving hot and heavy over her flesh. And when he entered her again she forgot all thoughts anyway.

He flipped her over in his arms until she was sitting astride him, his hands curving from her hips to her waist and up higher, till he took both breasts in his hands, cherishing them, taking pleasure in them, celebrating their fullness, his thumbs rolling the pebbled peaks of her nipples between them.

And then he moved inside her and she gasped, her back arching. The feeling was different, fuller, deeper than anything before, and pleasure roiled within her. Pleasure and aching heat. He moved again, his hands on her hips, guiding her along his length till she was almost at his limit and then letting her fill herself with him again. He let her find the rhythm, sometimes achingly slow, sometimes descending like a woman possessed. As she must be. Possessed by him.

Absorbing him.

Loving him.

It was back, she realised on a gasp, and worse than before. She'd been but a teenager, totally inexperienced in the world, when she'd first fallen in love. Now she should know better than to fall in love with a man like Alex Koutoufides. But that still didn't stop her.

Damn her, but she loved him. She wanted him. Every part of him.

And it frightened her, this new knowledge of loving him, of new experiences and new sensations. Of his hard length even now swelling inside her, and how much power she held over him. She watched the sweat break out on his brow as he searched for control even while she battled to retain hers against the mounting forces that felt as if they were trying to split her apart. With a sudden cry he grabbed for her hips, flipping her underneath him and lunging into her, each time bringing her closer and closer to that shattering conclusion she craved, taking her there in one final thrust and going with her into that gasping, yawning chasm of release.

Saskia felt a mounting sickness inside her. After a night of making love and a morning spent waking up to it, he'd organised a jet to take them to London. They had finally touched down in the evening, too late for anything but a late dinner in the plush hotel restaurant. An appointment had been requested with Sir Rodney first thing in the morning and if all went well there Saskia planned to visit with her father later in the afternoon. Hopefully the news would be good.

Now, Saskia toyed with her wine glass, turning the stem between her fingers, looking absently out of the large picture windows overlooking Regents Park while she waited for Alex to return from making a call. If she received this promotion she'd be based near London permanently, her time primarily taken up with her new role with the magazine, her weekends taken up with caring for her father. And whatever was happening here between her and Alex would be over.

Thank goodness.

How she'd managed to even look at herself in the mirror this morning she didn't know. She'd thrown herself upon him like a desperate virgin incensed that he'd rejected her once before. She'd fallen for the man who'd destroyed her father's life.

How could she even face her father after that?

Cramps squeezed what little she'd eaten into a tight ball inside her.

Thank God this would soon be over. Alex had been tense all day. He wanted her gone just as much as she needed to flee. Why else would he be pursuing any chance to help her win her job? He was pulling out all the stops to ensure she had a chance for this promotion.

Alex returned to the table and smiled tensely down at her, apologising for taking so long as he lifted a bottle of champagne from the ice bucket and filled both their glasses. And in spite of the churning in her tummy she couldn't help an uneasy smile back. Because right this minute it didn't matter if he didn't want her beyond tonight. Already muscles she'd thought well spent made themselves felt, making their interest clear to her in a way that brought heat and colour to her cheeks. She had this night to look forward to—why spoil it?

He picked up his flute and slanted it towards her. 'It's confirmed. We meet Sir Rodney at eleven. Here's to a successful outcome. Here's to getting what you want.'

They touched glasses, the expensive tink of crystal against crystal a total contrast to the sensation of her stomach crunching into more knots.

How could she get what she really wanted when she didn't know what she wanted herself?

She sipped from her glass, tiny beads sparkling in the fine wine, her heart strangely heavy.

'Would you like to do something after the meeting? Maybe take in a river cruise or visit a gallery?'

'Thanks,' she said, 'but I've got plans for the afternoon already.'

Surprise gave way to a resigned shrug. 'I see.' He picked up his glass. 'What have you arranged?'

She took a deep breath. 'I'm visiting with my father.'

His glass stilled at his mouth, mid swallow, before slowly he replaced it on the table. 'Your father lives here? In London? When did that happen?'

Her eyes challenged him. 'Where did you think he lived? Still back in Sydney? He came with me when I got my scholarship to the London School of Economics. Did you really think I'd leave him alone in Sydney after everything that had happened? He couldn't wait to get away and make a fresh start.'

'And has he?' Alex demanded, his tone suddenly aggressive. 'What kind of "fresh start" has he made?'

Saskia twisted her serviette in her lap. He had tried—at least in those first years. He'd started out in a new country with determination and a whole new zest for living. But when proposal after proposal for new businesses had been knocked back, with partners pulling out at the last minute, finance continually declined, then so had he. His dreams to start another business curtailed, he'd searched for employment. But jobs for aging executives with experience half a world away were thin on the ground. Soon he hadn't even been trying, and it had been only then that she'd found him spending more time with the betting pages than the employment guide. Before long she had discovered he'd gambled what little they'd had left clean away, and the debts were already mounting.

'These last few years,' she admitted, 'it's been hard.'

'*Life's* hard.'

Her sadness evaporated in an instant, incinerated in the harshness of his pronouncement. 'I certainly didn't expect any sympathy from you! Not after you'd done your bit—pulling the company out from under his feet the way you did.'

'In exactly the same way he ruined *my* father's business. If he could dish it out, you'd think he might have been able to take it.'

She stood up to go, placing her napkin on the table. 'I really don't want to sit here and listen to this.'

Alex snared her wrist in one hand. 'Sit down,' he snapped. Then, softer, 'Please. I shouldn't have said anything. Let's not argue tonight.'

She stood there, torn between leaving his man with a hatred for her father she couldn't understand—a man she shouldn't be with, not if loyalty to her father meant anything. And yet the very thought of walking away from Alex right now almost ripped her in two.

In the end it was only the thought that she would have to leave him anyway, and soon, that allowed her to sit down. That and the fact she still needed his help tomorrow with the board if she was going to be able to help her father at all. But soon enough she'd never see Alex again. Soon enough he'd be gone from her life. What was one more night of passion to steal before then?

A tense meal stretched into tense coffee, stretched into a tense journey to the penthouse suite. Alex hadn't even made a pretence of booking two rooms for them this trip, and both of them knew what was in store.

Inside the suite's welcoming lobby he pulled her straight into his arms. She came reluctantly, like a piece of board, all angles and stiffness and attitude. And then his mouth met hers and he felt the resistance drain out of her, her lips parting and welcoming, his tongue meeting hers, tasting and duelling. And somewhere in the midst of it their mutual resentment gave way to mutual desperate need, and clothes were tackled, peeled off, shucked. He manoeuvred her through to the magnificent bedroom and they hit the four-poster bed, a frenzy of entwined lips and tangled limbs and frantic grabs for air. He barely had time to sheath himself before he was inside her, driving, thrusting, seeking that place that wiped all others away, finding it in her and spinning them both over the abyss.

For a while they lay gasping together, their bodies humming, their senses slowly returning to something approaching normality. 'Stay there,' he said, kissing her forehead before easing away, padding to the bathroom and turning on the gold-plated taps over the large oval-shaped bathtub. A bottle of hotel bubble bath followed. When he came back he found her wrapped in a fluffy robe at the dressing table, removing her jewellery.

He growled and caught hold of her and spun her towards him, taking hold of the tied ends of the robe and unlooping them. He let the sides fall open, exposing a long window of shimmering skin, of womanly curves and golden blonde curls, and he felt himself start to get hard all over again.

She watched him with those green, green eyes, watched him drink her in, watched him take his fill of her and smile. And he saw sadness in those green eyes, mixed in with her desire. And he saw his own desire reflected back at him.

And then he buried his mouth on her neck, where her pulse jumped ragged for him. 'I'm running a bath for us,' he said. 'So you won't be needing this.' He let the robe drop from her shoulders, leaving her naked in his arms, his hands scanning her surface, cherishing every dip, memorising every curve.

'You go ahead,' he said at last, while he knew he was still capable of letting her go. 'I'll get us a drink.'

Still he turned to watch her go across the carpet, the gentle sway of her hips like a seduction in itself. He breathed in a groan and threw his head back, reefing his hands through his hair. She was going to walk out of his life the same way she'd just walked to the bathroom.

Eight years after he'd sent her packing, he was about to lose her again. And he was doing his utmost to ensure it happened.

Eight years ago he'd been sure about his decision. Now he didn't know what to think.

But he couldn't let her just walk out of his life as if she'd never been there. He'd been given a second chance—a second chance to get things right, not merely a second chance to make love to her. What the hell was wrong with him? Why hadn't he been able to see that before?

He *would* make things right. For both of them. Starting now.

She didn't have to take that job. Whatever it was that meant so much to her about it, he'd give her that tenfold. She didn't want his money, she'd made that clear, but he could make up for what had happened in the past with more than mere cash. She could come and live with him. She wouldn't need to scrimp and worry about money again. They could pretend the past had never happened. They could start afresh.

And he'd take care of her.

Starting tonight.

A bottle of champagne stood chilling in a crystal ice bucket on a silver tray, two crystal flutes alongside. He popped the cork on the champagne, filling the flutes only halfway. He'd just picked up the bottle and glasses when a flashing light caught his eye. Someone had left a message while they were out.

He almost didn't bother picking it up, but if Sir Rodney and his cronies had changed the appointment time they would be better off finding out tonight, before the two of them embarked on what he expected would be another long night of sex. It wouldn't do to be late for the meeting, even though now his own agenda had taken a slight change of direction. If he played his cards right tonight, Saskia would no longer have to plead for a chance at this promotion. She'd be handing in her resignation. He put the bottle down and picked up the receiver, pressing the message bank button as he happily contemplated tomorrow's meeting.

'Saskia!'

He blinked as he recognised the voice, a prickly suspicion crawling through him, congealing in his gut. Why the hell would Marla be calling Saskia? He focused on the message she'd left.

'I have such exciting news. They've made an offer on my memoirs. They recommended I get an agent straight away, so I need your help. When are you back? Call me when you get a chance. I can't believe it—they're going to publish my book! And I owe it all to you!'

CHAPTER NINE

THE bath was liquid heaven, the bubbles up to her chin, the spa jets gently massaging muscles sore in places from abilities she had never dreamed possible. She closed her eyes and let her head loll back against the rim. But she wasn't about to go to sleep. Not a chance. Soon Alex would join her, and another chapter in her sexual awakening would begin. And in the slippery oil-scented water she was very much looking forward to this particular chapter.

Tonight she wouldn't think about anything but what he would teach her and what she would learn. Tomorrow there would be time enough for recriminations.

Saskia sensed rather than heard the door open. She opened her eyes and looked around, expecting him to be still naked, expecting him to join her. But he was wearing jeans and a buttoned shirt, and the look on his face was dark thunder. She frowned, lifting herself a little higher in the water.

'Alex?'

'You bitch,' he snarled. 'How the hell did you think you'd get away with it?'

She sat right up now, turning around to face him, ignoring the sluice of water and the slide of bubbles from her skin. 'Alex, what's wrong?'

'All the time you demanded to be trusted. All the time you pretended to be something you're not. All that crap about a profile. All that rubbish about suddenly not being in the running for the promotion. It was all one big con. There never was any promotion. There never was any competition. It was all one big cover-up for what you were really doing.'

'I don't understand.' She pushed herself up and out of the bath, securing one of the enormous bath sheets around her while he continued to stand like some gunslinger looking to shoot her down. 'What are you talking about?'

'Marla's memoirs are what I'm talking about!'

Fear sent shivers down her spine. He'd been bound to find out some time, but why now? Why now, before Marla had had a chance to speak to him about it herself? 'How did you find out?'

His lips turned into a sneer. 'And you're in so deep you can't even deny it.'

She shook her head, grabbed another smaller towel to wipe away the foam that still clung to her shoulders and hair. 'Why should I deny it? She asked me to read them.'

He grabbed the towel and whipped it out of her reach, forcing her to focus on him and him alone. 'You're lying! You've been stalking her from the start.'

'You don't know what you're talking about. Marla asked me to read them. So I did, and they were good. And I passed them onto a friend of mine who works for a publisher in New York. Like Marla also asked me to do.'

'I told you to stay away from her!'

'And I did. She sought *me* out. I didn't go looking for her.'

'You're lying.'

'It's the truth! Don't blame me. Blame yourself. Marla and

I might have been confined to different cell blocks, but you were the one who had us living in the same prison compound.'

'You promised me in New York that you'd stay away from her.'

'No! I promised you that this profile would be about you!' she reminded him. 'Besides, I'd already told Marla I'd read her manuscript, and I wasn't about to break a promise I'd made to her.'

'You didn't tell me.'

'Why the hell should I? I knew what you'd say, how you'd react. So did Marla. But she pleaded with me to read it and I did.' She glared up at him, waiting for the next explosion. 'So what's happened?' she asked. Sick of being confined to the bathroom, she shoved past him and made her way to the dressing room, needing the security of clothes. She couldn't hold this conversation wearing only a towel.

'Did Marla call?'

'She left you a message,' he responded, following her. 'Some sleazy publisher has offered her a contract to publish them.'

She spun around, her hands full of clothes, the significance of his message overshadowing his insult. 'They want to make her an offer? But that's great news. She must be so excited. Surely you can see how wonderful an opportunity this is for her?'

'What I can see,' Alex said, coming towards her so fast he seemed to rise up like a mountain over her, 'is that you've succeeded in getting my sister to splash the sordid details of her entire life to the papers.'

'This isn't the papers, and it's not about sordid details. If what you say is true, and I hope it is for her sake, then it's a book deal. She's actually scored the heady achievement of selling her first book. Do you have any idea how rare it is to have your first book published?'

'Sleaze will always find a market.'

'How *dare* you say that? This is your sister's writing we're talking about. And if you bothered to read it you'd see it's an amazingly well-written account of one person's life and her struggle to find herself. *In her words*. Noone else's. And it's funny and witty and touching and wise. Did you know your sister was so talented? I doubt it. I bet you didn't even know your sister was a writer.'

His eyes slid away and she knew she'd hit a raw nerve.

'Marla's a gifted writer,' she continued, 'and now she might even have the start of a career. Don't you want that for her? Don't you want her to have a real life? Or are you so determined to keep up this big brother act, keep her locked away, that you can't even see what's good for her any more? Can't you see that's why she breaks out? Because she wants freedom—not to be treated like a child!'

'She needs my support.'

'No, she needs her freedom. You keep her locked away in a gilded prison. No wonder when she breaks out she seeks every bit of attention she can find. You've got her so locked away she doesn't even know who she is.'

'And you think *you* know what's good for her?' His face was severe, his mouth twisted, and Saskia knew she'd hurt him.

'Look, I know you care for her. She's your sister and you love her. But maybe you should back off a bit. Maybe you should give her a bit more responsibility and freedom. I know she wants it.'

'And splattering her life in print is the way to do it? Why couldn't you leave her alone? I told you to leave her alone!'

'Alex, listen—'

'Marla was fine until your family came along. What business do you have in trying to ruin her life? Don't you think your father's done enough to her already?'

His words shocked her into silence, and he stood over her, his chest heaving, the words hanging between them like a damnation. Why should he hold such deep-seated hatred for her father? Sure, their families had history, but so did just about every other family engaged in business in Sydney. It was an occupational hazard.

'Look, we both know my father took over your family's business. And I know it must have been difficult for your family. But it was such a long time ago. Maybe it's time you got over it.'

He laughed—the sound of the devil, evil and poisoned with acrimony—and fear flared out from her spine. 'I'm not talking about the takeover,' he sneered, his face now only inches from her own.

Dread rooted her to the spot. But if it wasn't the takeover… 'Then, what?'

'I'm talking about when your father raped my sister!'

Cold shock drenched through her, dousing her in disbelief. She was unable to speak, unable to respond, the shaking of her head the only movement she was capable of.

'You don't believe me? You don't believe your precious father could do such a thing?'

'No,' she protested. It was too revolting, too ugly to have any measure of truth. Dear God, not her father. It was a lie. It had to be.

'Believe it,' he said. 'Your dear sweet father wasn't content to strip my father's business bare. He decided to strip Marla of her virginity as well.'

'No! It can't be possible.'

'More than possible. It happened. And your father waved the fact he'd stolen Marla's virginity in front of my father like a trophy.'

'It can't be true.'

'She was *fifteen* years old!'

Every revelation was worse than the one before. She cowered before him, reeling from his accusations as if they were body blows. Marla had been a teenager—little more than a child. It couldn't be true. It just couldn't.

Until she remembered the memoirs—how Marla had lost her virginity at the age of fifteen—to a much older man.

Could that man have been Saskia's own father?

Could he have acted that way? Her own father? How could he have done it? Surely he could never have committed such a horrendous act, only then to turn around and flaunt the fact in front of Marla's father? It would have destroyed them.

But then, it *had* destroyed them, hadn't it?

What had Alex told her? His parents had never recovered from the shock of the takeover. Only now she could see that it hadn't been the takeover that had destroyed them, it had been despair at what had happened to their young daughter.

Why else would Alex hate her father so much? He must know it was true. And so far nothing else made sense. Nothing else fitted.

She'd always known her father had prided himself on his ruthless business skills, but she'd never seen him in that light. Saskia must have been only about one year old at the time, and to her as a child her father had been her gruff teddy bear, who'd sent her into fits of laughter by teasing her with his whiskers when wishing her goodnight.

How could the same man who had tickled her and kissed her goodnight do something so hideous to someone else's daughter? She shuddered. Had he kissed her goodnight after what he'd done to Marla? Oh, God, she hoped not.

With a cry of grief and disgust she bolted for the bathroom, losing what little she'd managed to eat of her Michelin three-star meal.

He stalked up behind her, throwing her a towel that she grabbed hold of and clutched to her mouth. 'I know,' he said, his voice hard and remorseless. 'It turns my stomach too.'

She was shaking, her body too weak to stand, her breathing ragged. 'Alex,' she croaked. 'I had no idea. I didn't know.'

'So now you do. And now you know why I didn't want you having anything to do with Marla from the start.'

'You were protecting me from discovering what my father had done.'

'I was protecting *her*! This was always about Marla, about keeping her safe.'

Oh no, she suddenly thought. *Marla*. The woman had trusted her, had sought out her help. She looked up at him, 'Does she know? I mean, about me... I mean...'

'That you're *his* daughter? Of course she doesn't! Why the hell else would she have anything to do with you?'

'I don't know what to say,' she said, blotting her face on the towel, wishing it could soak up the horror, wishing it could mop up the past.

'Then do me a favour and don't say anything.' His face had moved beyond fury. The heat had dispersed and now it was ice that met her gaze—cold, unforgiving ice that chilled her heart and soul.

'You know, I actually believed we could forget the past because I thought you were different. For a while there you had me so taken with sleeping with you I even forgot who your father was.' He laughed, this time a self-deprecating sound that smacked of how much of a fool he thought he'd been. 'But you're no different than he is—preying on the naïve and vulnerable for your own sick purpose. Now I can see you're truly your father's daughter. You two really deserve each other.'

He disappeared once more into the suite. A few seconds later she heard him talking, barking orders into the phone.

She stood, still shaky, and washed her face, shocked at how pale her skin looked in the mirror. She saw movement behind her and turned. Alex had his leather briefcase and suit bag in his hands, and her heart—something she hadn't thought could get any lower—took a dive.

'You're leaving?'

'I'm moving to another suite. I'll be flying back first thing tomorrow. I'll ship over anything you left.'

'What about tomorrow morning's meeting?'

'Oh, come on, Saskia. Enough's enough. You don't expect me to believe that rubbish still. You've got what you wanted. You've already got Marla bending over backwards to spill her guts to the tabloids, or wherever else you want her to, even if I do manage to get that manuscript back. You don't have to convince me now. It's too late.'

She thought she saw something move across his eyes—a sad look, almost of regret—but it was fleeting and too quickly blinked away. And too easily misinterpreted, she thought, knowing that looking for something in his eyes, hoping for it, would not make it so.

Like he said, it was too late.

And it was no wonder he didn't want anything to do with her. She was a constant reminder of what her father had done.

'Oh, and when you see your father tomorrow…'

She waited a few seconds, then, 'Yes?'

'Let him know that he's the only man I ever felt like murdering. Tell him that under the circumstances he ended up getting off lightly.'

Saskia closed her eyes against the bitterness of his parting jibe, and by the time she'd opened them he'd gone. Seconds later she heard the cushioned thunk of the suite's solid front door closing.

He was gone.

Again.

For the second time in her life he was casting her aside. And for the second time in her life she felt as if her insides had been ripped out of her body, shredded into ribbons and hung out to dry.

CHAPTER TEN

THE meeting with Sir Rodney and the board had gone as well as could be expected. At least that was what Saskia told herself, trying to find some positive angle as she stood outside the Snapmedia building, wrapping her coat more tightly around her and battling back tears under the grey, sleet-threatening sky.

Because, in all seriousness, what had she expected? The board were bound to have been unimpressed with the fact that the man who'd insisted they all get together for a meeting to convince them their engagement had been a farce from the start hadn't even bothered to show up.

If she'd slept last night, if she hadn't lain awake in the empty suite, being tormented by the awful knowledge that her father was not the man she thought he was, that he was suddenly a stranger, then she might have been able to argue her case. But she'd been shattered by both the news and her sleepless night, and part of her wondered if she'd even wanted to fight anyway.

In the end the board had conceded that if she could get her profile in within the week there was a slim chance she might still be considered for the position, but it would have to stack up against Carmen's excellent in-depth report.

She'd almost laughed in their faces. How could she turn in a profile when her subject had just walked out on her? She didn't stand a chance. But then, why did she even need a chance?

Why did she need this job to pay for a house for her father when right now she wasn't even sure she ever wanted to see him again?

She sniffed against the heavy cold air, blinking away the tears from her scratchy eyes as engaged cab after engaged cab cruised past. Of course she wanted to see him—he was her father, after all. The only father she'd ever have. And he was old and frail, and he had no one else to take care of him, and she had no one else to take care of.

But if it were true…

If he'd committed such an unforgivable act…

Oh, where *were* all the empty cabs in London?

She rubbed her hands together, wishing she'd worn gloves and suddenly missing Alex, with his limousines and jets on tap. He turned travel into an art form, not this battle for survival.

Finally she managed to coax a black cab to the kerb. She pulled open the back door and jumped inside.

'Where to, luv?' asked the driver.

It was warm in the cab, much warmer than outside, and it took her a moment to register that she needed to make a decision—now.

She took a deep breath and gave him her father's address.

Twenty minutes and half a lifetime of dread later the taxi pulled up opposite her father's dingy block of flats.

He's an old man, she told herself as she climbed the stairs to the second floor.

He was still the same old man she'd spoken to a week ago.

And, whatever else he'd done, he was still her father. But it was hard to convince herself of that—so hard to feel warm for the man who'd tucked her in at night at the same time. God only knew what else had been happening.

It was after the third time she'd knocked that she started regretting the fact she hadn't let him know she was coming. But then she hadn't known what she was going to say. And what *could* she say?—*Hi, Dad, what was it like to have sex with Alex Koutoufides's sister?*

Maybe it was just as well he wasn't home. Maybe she wasn't ready for this. But then, where was he? The last time she'd rung he'd been too ill to leave the flat.

The door of the adjoining flat opened and a woman peered out.

'Mrs Sharpe,' Saskia said, relieved to see the neighbour. 'I've come to visit my father, but he's not answering. Do you know where he might be?'

Enid Sharpe's face creased into wrinkles deep enough for caverns and her bird-like frame shuffled out through the door towards her. 'Oh, Saskia, my luvvy, haven't you heard?'

Alex was in a foul mood by the time he got back to Tahoe, and it didn't help matters when Marla came outside to meet the car, the smile on her face broader than he'd seen in years. She rushed up to kiss him on the cheek, and then looked around the car, puzzled.

'Where's Saskia?'

'London,' he snapped, snatching up his bags from the boot of the car himself, before the driver could collect them.

'But why? When's she coming back?'

'She won't be,' he said, noticing Jake standing by the door, waiting. He nodded. 'Jake.'

'Good to have you back, boss.'

You won't think that when I'm done with you. 'Meet me in

my office,' he told him. They had a few matters to discuss concerning Marla's secret liaisons. 'Fifteen minutes.'

Marla trailed him through to the massive timber-beamed living area. 'But…'

He turned around alongside the stone fireplace, ready to snap her head off, and then something struck him as different about her. 'What have you done to yourself?' he asked. 'You look different.'

She reached a tentative hand to her hair and shrugged. 'I coloured it, that's all. Do you like it?'

What was not to like? It was honey-gold, just the way he liked it. Just like… He growled, clamping down on the thought.

'I got your message,' he said. 'I know about the book.'

She blinked. 'Oh?'

'And I want you to know I'll do everything I can to get it back.'

'What do you mean?' Her hands clutched his arm. 'They want to buy it. It's going to be published.'

'Not if I can help it.'

'No! You don't understand. Saskia said—'

He shrugged off her hands. 'I don't care what Saskia said!'

She stood watching him, her breathing fast and furious. 'How did you find out? I left that message for Saskia, and she wouldn't have told you. I asked for Saskia's room…' Her eyes suddenly widened. 'You two shared a room. You slept with her, didn't you?'

Alex swung his bags around and resumed walking past the fireplace towards the master bedroom wing.

'You slept with Saskia. I *knew* you would. It was obvious you wanted to. Is that why she hasn't returned my calls? But what did you say to her? What did you do to her to make her stay in London?'

He spun around, incensed at what his sister was saying—

doubly incensed at what she'd perceived. 'I told her from the very beginning to stay away from you. But she couldn't, could she? She pretended to be here to interview me, when all along she was angling to get the dirt on you. I trusted her to keep away from you, and she couldn't.'

'You've never trusted anybody in your life!'

'She told me she was here to do my profile.'

'And she was.'

'Then how did she end up selling *your* story?'

'Because I sought her out! I saw her walking along the lake shore in the early morning and I went down to talk to her. I liked her. It was nice to talk to another woman for a change, and that's when I asked if she'd be willing to read my manuscript.'

'I'm sure that's how it was.'

'She told me you wouldn't like it. I had to beg her to read it. I even had to pretend it was written by someone else. She didn't believe me for a minute, though. And I know she was thinking it was going to be hopeless, and she really didn't want to know, but I was desperate. I made her take it.'

Alex looked at his sister, weighing up her words. Marla had done plenty of things in her time that he didn't like, but she'd never lied to him. And wasn't that exactly what Saskia had told him—that Marla had sought her out?

But so what? It didn't matter in the scheme of things. She was still who she was. Nothing would ever change that.

'It doesn't change the fact that you have to pull that manuscript. We have to get it back.'

Marla crossed her arms and stamped her heel down hard. 'What if I don't want to?'

'Then it's getting pulled anyway. You know I'm only doing what's best for you.'

'No, you're not. How can you know what's best for me?

Have you ever *asked* me what I'd like? And, given the way you've obviously treated Saskia over this, you don't even know what's best for you. How can you possibly think you're any judge of what might be good for someone else?'

Alex sighed and raked the fingers of one hand through his hair. He was tired and hungry and he'd had enough of women lately—especially women who couldn't see what was obvious and yet imagined all sorts of other things. But maybe he'd come on too strong all the same. There was no point taking out his frustrations over what had happened with Saskia on Marla.

'Look, I just want you to be happy, okay?'

'Fine. That makes two of us.'

'Then there's no point publishing a whole lot of stuff that's going to hit the fan big time.'

'How do you know that's going to happen? You haven't even read it.'

'Come on, Marla. Since when has anyone published anything about you that hasn't caused trouble?'

'But *I* wrote this. Don't you even trust me to get it right?'

'This isn't about trust—'

'Yes, it is! I'm nearly forty years old, and still you don't trust me to tell my story my way and not screw it up. If you just talked to Saskia—'

'*No!* I will not be talking to Saskia—and if you know what's good for you, neither will you.'

'And yet it was okay for you to sleep with her?'

Breath hissed through his teeth. 'You don't understand. You don't know what kind of person she is.'

'I know she's not the gutter press you'd like to make her out to be.'

'It's not just what she is; it's *who* she is.'

'Because she's Victor Prentice's daughter?'

With his brain still fogged from too much travel and too little sleep he had to take a second to assimilate what she'd just said.

'You knew?'

'Of course I knew! I mean, not straight away, but it wasn't too hard to work out—not with her photo and her name plastered all over every paper in town.'

'But her father…'

'You don't have to remind me who her father is or what her father did! I was there—remember?'

'You were only fifteen!'

'And you were only twelve! What could you have really known about it at the time? I wish you'd never found out. I wish Dad had never said anything to you.'

'I knew something was going on even before he did. So many hushed conversations. So many tears. And when I found out he'd raped you I wanted to kill him. I swore I'd have my revenge for what he did.'

She looked at him open-mouthed. 'What did you just say? He *raped* me? Is that what you've believed all these years?'

'He took your virginity. You were only a teenager. What would you call it?'

'I'd call it sex. I'd call it satisfying a mutual need.'

'Tsou!' The word exploded from him as he reeled away. When he turned he was pointing his finger at her like an accusation. 'He was old enough to be your father! Why would you feel any such need with *him*? How would you even know what you needed?'

She shrugged. 'Who can explain attraction? He was older, and I thought he was so dashing and powerful. I was drawn to him, and curious about sex. And he was so lonely and sad—with no wife and a tiny child. I guess I felt sorry for him.'

'But why would you agree to do such a thing?'

'I didn't agree. *He* did.'

She gave him time to let the words sink in—time that he desperately needed to make sense of it all.

'But that would mean…'

'Exactly,' she said. 'I *asked* him to make love to me. I chose him to show me what it was to be a woman. I know what he did was wrong, and so did he, but I begged him—even forced myself on him, if you must know.' She tilted her head, her brow furrowed slightly. 'Is this why you've been so against Saskia from the start? It wasn't just that she was a journalist? It was because she was Victor's daughter? How could you possibly hold that against her, when she was still in nappies at the time?'

He reached his arms up, pushing his neck back against his knotted fingers. 'It doesn't matter. He still had sex with you. He had no right—'

'Forget about Victor! You have to let this hatred go, Alex! It's history. Besides, Victor's little more than a broken man now. He's frail, and needs constant help.' She stopped when she saw his double-take. 'You mean you didn't know? Didn't you speak to Saskia at all while you had her here? Or were you too busy angling her into your bed? Why else do you think she's so desperate for this promotion of hers? It's the only way she's going to be able to afford decent care for him.'

'*Theos!*' he said, closing his eyes as he spun around, feeling suddenly ill. He couldn't have managed this more badly if he'd tried.

'What have you done?' Marla came closer, put a hand to his arm. 'Didn't you go over there to help her? What happened?'

He looked down at his sister, but he saw nothing but the pain on Saskia's face—the pain he'd savagely inflicted when he'd accused her father of committing the most hideous of crimes, of raping his sister. He heard Marla's rapid intake of breath, registered her shocked withdrawal.

'Oh, my God! You didn't tell her… Please say you didn't tell her that…?'

He shook his head. He couldn't deny it. Just as he couldn't deny he'd sent her packing for the second time. He'd used her and insulted her and then thrown her to the wolves, discarding her like a piece of dirt. And he'd felt so righteous. In spite of everything there had been moments in that hotel room in London when he'd wanted to keep her, wanted to have her in his bed and by his side, when he hadn't wanted to let her go. But at the last minute he'd been saved from those weak urges by hearing Marla's news and proving he'd been right not to trust Saskia all along.

What the hell had he done?

Alex stood in his study, his hands in his pockets, gazing unseeingly out of the floor-to-ceiling cedar-framed windows. He knew what the view looked like from here. He knew every tree and boulder leading down to the lake. He knew every mountain rising on the far distant shore.

So why today did everything look so different?

The morning was sharp and crisp, the lake water so still and clear he could see right down into the boulder strewn shallows. He'd given up on sleep and spent most of the night in his study, catching up on business he'd neglected over the last few days.

But his mind hadn't been on business either.

Sleep eluded him. Business escaped him. Only one thing stood as stark and clear as the towering pines that framed his view. Only one thing accounted for the sick feeling in his empty stomach.

He'd been wrong.

Totally, completely, unforgivably wrong.

And that was just about his sister.

For years he'd thought he was protecting her, wrapping her up in cotton wool, trying to keep her safe and wondering why she'd escape his protective custody at every opportunity. Who could blame her? He'd never trusted her. He'd never let her find her own way. He'd taken her mistakes as signals that he should make all the decisions, not that she just needed the space and time to learn.

It was a wonder she still deigned to call him her brother.

But if he'd done wrong by Marla, his own sister, then what he'd done to Saskia was one thousand times worse.

He'd misjudged her, he'd mistrusted her, he'd damned her to hell—a hell that he himself had crafted for her—and then he'd left her there to rot.

Hell, if he ran his business this way he'd be bankrupt in a minute.

And wasn't that word appropriate?

Bankrupt.

Morally and ethically, when it came to Saskia, he lacked the most basic resources. He'd misjudged her from the start because of who she was and what she reminded him of. He'd misjudged her motives, he'd mistrusted her, he'd refused to believe her. And when he'd learned about Marla selling her memoirs all his vile prejudices had thrown a party and celebrated. He'd been right all along!

And yet he'd been so wrong.

He'd taken the moral high ground, thinking that ground was solid, not realising how thin a crust he was standing on.

And that crust had crumbled into chalk dust when he'd learned the truth about her.

She hadn't lied to him. She hadn't betrayed his trust. She'd recognised things about his relationship with his sister that he'd been blind to, that he hadn't wanted to hear. And she'd come here, dealing with the one person she'd never wanted to see in her life again, not for personal gain but to ensure she could care for her father.

What a damned fool he was! He fisted his hands to his forehead as the trees, the lake, the mountains all faded away before him. All he could see was her body slumped on the bathroom floor, her hand clutching a towel to her face, her eyes large and fearful like a wounded animal's. He'd dumped the news of what her father had done to his sister like a victory. It had been his *pièce de résistance* and he'd made the most of it, twisting it like a long, sharp-bladed knife in deep.

He'd trashed her father. He'd trashed her career by not staying to support her in front of her board. He'd trashed her life. And then he'd coldly walked away.

He'd had his second chance with her. He'd had a chance to put things between them to rights. And for a brief time he'd thought he could—that they might even have a life together, a future.

But he'd blown his precious chance sky-high.

Now there was no hope.

Saskia squirmed to wakefulness in the vinyl chair, its wooden arms cutting into her legs where they tucked under her. She opened her eyes and looked over at her father, hoping to see some improvement. Her heart sank as rapidly as it had risen.

No change.

After three days at his bedside she knew what to look for. After three days she was beginning to wonder if the coma that had claimed him after his inoperable brain stem haemorrhage was ever going to let him go. Would he ever be able to breathe without that tube down his throat and a machine to fill his chest with air?

'It could be five days before he wakes up,' the doctors had warned her. 'Or it could be five months. And even then…'

She clamped her eyes shut, trying to keep back the glum prognosis they'd issued, but the painful truth seeped through. She had to be ready, they'd told her. Even if he woke up he'd need months, maybe even years of rehabilitation. And that was the up side.

She didn't want to think about any of it. She'd already tied herself up in knots thinking, but right now what was the alternative? Trawling over the train wreck of the last couple of weeks with Alex? Not likely. There was no joy down that path. Only self-recrimination. Because for the second time in her life she'd offered herself to the man she'd fancied herself in love with. And for the second time she'd been discarded like something stinking stuck to his shoe.

But how utterly stupid of her was it that it had been the same man both times?

Hadn't she learned *anything* the first time around?

Saskia looked over at her father. The machine alongside him was ensuring the constant rise and fall of his chest, keeping him alive until such time as he could breathe on his own again. She looked at his creased sunken cheeks and his closed eyes as he slept, and he just looked like an old man.

When she'd gone to see him at the flat she'd been sick to the stomach over how she would greet him. What would she say? How could she believe what Alex had told her was true, and that her own father was capable of such an act? Because she was so very scared it was.

But now he was lying there in a coma, critically ill, possibly dying. Now only one fact mattered.

He was her father.

The only father she had.

And, God forgive her, she still loved him.

Tears slid down her cheeks. So what kind of person did that make her? Maybe Alex had been right. Maybe she truly was her father's daughter.

The door swung open and a nurse bustled into the room, flashing her a compassionate smile as she breezed by to check her patient's vitals. 'Beautiful day outside, Miss Prentice, but they're predicting it'll rain later. Maybe you should grab a cup of tea and get some fresh air while you can?'

Saskia stretched, and eased her feet into her shoes.

'Maybe you're right,' she agreed, swiping away at her own precipitation. There was precious little she could do here.

It was dark when she made it back to her tiny one-bedroom flat, bone-weary and wanting nothing more taxing than to lose herself in a long hot bath. She'd been at the hospital for five and a half days, refusing to go further than the gardens outside, refusing to leave her father's side for any length of time. He had nobody else—what if he woke up?

But the doctors were right. It was time to go home.

She swung the door open and let herself inside, snapping on the light. A neat pile of mail sat on the dresser and she gave silent thanks—as usual, her landlady had been keeping an eye on the place while she'd been away. Then she turned to see an untidier stack of boxes filling one half of her living room.

She looked at them, blinking as she moved closer, checking for the forwarding address.

Tahoe. That explained it. Alex had said he'd send her things. But why so many? She'd left barely anything there. And what she had left she really didn't care if she never saw again.

She slit through the tape on the first box and peeled back the flaps. Clothes. The outfits he'd bought her in Sydney— the boutique full of clothes he'd had delivered so she could look the part of his fiancée. Clothes she'd never considered hers. The beautiful silk-chiffon dress she'd worn at the airport that first day ran through her fingers. The ballgown she'd worn in New York was folded like treasure, and everything else was in between. There were clothes she'd never worn, and shoes and bags and underwear.

She sat back on her heels and contemplated it all, absorbing the shock of her discoveries, trying to come to terms with the sheer cold-bloodedness of it all. She began to laugh.

It was funny, really. They'd never been her clothes, but he'd cleared the cupboards and sent everything to her as if they were. There was a box of ballgowns here! A boutique in a box there! 'Here a box, there a box,' she cried, whooping with laughter as an old nursery rhyme came to mind. 'Everywhere a box, box.'

She laughed and laughed, unable to stop the hysteria welling up inside. He'd dispensed with every trace of anything she might have breathed on, let alone touched. He'd wiped her existence from his life as if she'd never been there, and he'd bundled up and sent her the crumbs, so she would know just how little he wanted to be reminded of her.

It was too funny for words. Because what made Alex think for a moment that she wanted to be reminded of *him*?

And she kept on laughing, the tears streaming down her face, unable to recall later, when she'd dragged herself off to bed, just when it was that her laughter had given way to tears.

* * *

Twenty-four hours later she was functioning again. If you could call it that. The doorbell rang and she pulled her still wet hair into a ponytail, calling out that she was coming. The charity group she'd called to take away the boxes obviously hadn't wasted any time—but that was good. The sooner they were gone, the sooner she would be rid of the physical reminders of her time with Alex. The memories she knew would take longer.

She pulled open the door wide to let them in, and froze.

'Hello, Saskia.'

CHAPTER ELEVEN

SHE blinked, took a breath, but when she opened her eyes again it was still Alex standing on her threshold—and it was still an angry knot that was tangling up and pulling tight inside her.

'What are you doing here?'

'I came to see you.' She noticed the tight lines around his jaw, the lines between his brows. She took in the creases in his chambray shirt and the slight slump to his shoulders. He looked tired, maybe a little shattered. Even so, he looked a darned sight better than she knew she did.

'Aren't you going to ask me in?'

'Why should I?'

'Because we have to talk.'

She shook her head. 'I don't think so. I don't think there's anything left to say.'

Two men, one middle-aged and wearing overalls and one in his twenties in baggy jeans and a sloppy T-shirt, appeared behind Alex's shoulder, trying to get her attention. 'You got a pick-up for Charity Central, luv?'

'That's right,' she said. 'Just through here.'

Alex didn't move out of the way, she noticed with irritation. Instead he moved inside the room to let them pass.

She indicated the boxes with a sweep of her hand. 'All of these.'

Alex looked at the boxes and then back at her as the first box was lugged into strong arms and disappeared out through the door. 'Hang on a minute,' he protested. 'Aren't these…?'

She nodded. 'The very same.'

'Those clothes cost a fortune.'

'Your fortune,' she said. 'Not mine. But if you want them…'

The older man stopped midway to the door. 'So are they going or staying?'

'They're going.'

'They're staying.'

They spoke together.

The man huffed and put the box down, tapping his returning assistant on the arm to stop him picking up the next box. He drummed his fingers on the top of one box. 'So what's it to be, guv?' he said, deferring to Alex.

'I bought them for you,' he told Saskia accusingly.

'You bought them for your fake fiancée,' she replied, 'who is now surplus to requirements. As are these clothes. If I don't want them, and you don't want them, charity seems the perfect solution.'

'Fine,' Alex said, as if he was speaking through gritted teeth. 'Take them away.'

The man looked from one to the other and then nodded at his colleague. In three trips they'd cleared the living room, smiled their brief thanks and disappeared, before either of them could change their minds.

Saskia breathed a sigh of relief as she boiled the kettle for a long-deserved cup of tea. The boxes were gone. If only Alex, still occupying her living room as if he belonged there, could be dispensed with so easily.

'What was that all about?' he demanded, coming up behind her.

'This is my home,' she warned him, spinning around. 'You might rule the roost in your own fleet of houses and hotel rooms, but here, in this flat, what I say goes. Have you got that?'

She knew her voice sounded thready and weak. Hell, she *felt* thready and weak. But she couldn't just let him take control. 'Besides which,' she said, 'I don't actually remember inviting you in.'

His eyelids dipped, almost as if he was shutting out her protest. 'Nevertheless, I'm here.'

She turned to look at him, saw the hurt and ache that coursed through his eyes and suddenly wished she hadn't. What right did he have to want sympathy? After everything he'd done?

She turned back towards the bench, squeezing out her teabag, twisting it around a spoon to wring it out, and finally dropping it in the bin, all her actions running comfortingly on autopilot. Then she stirred in a heaped teaspoon full of sugar, just for good measure. Right now she could do with all the fortification she could get.

'What if I don't want you here? Did you consider that?'

'Oh, yes. I considered that.'

'And?'

'It wasn't an option.'

She laughed, feeling the lingering hysteria of the night before revisiting her. Only now that hysteria wanted to be magnified by his presence. 'Now, that sounds like the great Alexander Koutoufides.'

'No!' he said, grabbing her arm and sending boiling liquid sloshing over the rim floorwards, thankfully not over her.

She looked down at his hand, then up at him. 'Let me go.'

'I didn't come here to argue with you.'

'Then why *are* you here, Alex? What could you possibly want after all that's happened?'

He looked at her, and the longer he did so the more she wished she'd never let him in.

'I came to tell you I was sorry.'

She drank in a deep breath, plastering a thin smile to her face. 'Well, that makes up for just about everything, then.'

She forced herself to take a sip of her tea, knowing it was still too hot but needing something to do. Something that didn't involve interaction with him. And yet, even scalding hot, her tea was no competition for the heat generated by his presence.

'Marla told me she pursued you about getting her memoirs published. She said you didn't come after her at all.'

She barely threw him a glance. 'Oh, and isn't that what I'd told you already? I had the distinct impression you didn't believe me.'

Her accusation hung heavy in the air, but even though his head was bowed his eyes still held hers.

'I realise you don't have to make this easy for me, but I am trying to apologise.'

'Of course. Apology accepted,' she said brightly, clearly throwing him off balance. 'Now, if there's nothing more…' She gestured to the door.

'Dammit, Saskia! Of course there's more—lots more.' He wheeled away, forcing hands rigid like claws through his hair. When he spun back he was holding out his hands almost in supplication. 'I left London because I thought you'd betrayed my trust. I thought you'd gone behind my back to get whatever dirt you could on my sister. And when I spoke to Marla and found out how wrong I was, do you know how bad I felt?'

'No,' she said frankly. 'I have no idea.'

'I'd not only accused you of a lie,' he continued, ignoring her snippy reply, 'I'd abandoned you to face your boss and your board alone for probably the most important meeting of your career. How bad was it?'

'Oh, it was just peachy,' she told him. 'And they were good enough to give me a few days to get my profile in. Only problem was, my subject had walked out on me.' She shrugged as she took a sip of her sweet tea. *'C'est la vie.'*

'You'll get that job, if you still want it, with or without my profile.'

She looked up at him. 'How sweet of you to say so.' Then, just as his eyes were starting to relax and warm, she held one hand up and waved it in the air. 'But I don't care any more. I've decided to let Carmen have the job. She wants it so badly—frankly she must do, to have poured herself all over Drago the way she did—and she'll be good at it, I know.'

'Saskia, Carmen won't be needing that job.'

'What do you mean?'

'You haven't been listening to the news today? Drago Maiolo had a heart attack and drove his Ferrari through a barricade and over a cliff.'

'Oh God, that's awful. But what's that got to do with Carmen?'

'Carmen was in the car alongside him. She didn't stand a chance.'

It was too much. When would it all stop? She squeezed her eyes shut and swayed, letting herself slump into a chair. No matter how much Carmen had done to hurt her, nobody deserved to die like that.

'I'm sorry,' he told her. 'There was no easy way to say it. But don't you see? Now that job can be yours.'

She rested her forehead against her hand. 'And don't *you* see? I don't want that job!'

'But I thought you needed it for your father.'

She looked up at him, blinking blindly, her stomach yawning open into a whirlpool, sucking her down further into that dark, fetid, bottomless place.

'I know all about it,' he explained. 'Marla told me he was sick. She said you need money to fund his care. And she told me more—'

From somewhere she dredged the energy to stand. 'And now I'm supposed to believe you suddenly care about my father?' Her voice was accusing, though her senses were still reeling as she swiped up her barely touched cup and transferred it to the sink.

'Listen to me,' he urged. 'I spoke to Marla. What I said in that hotel—'

She spun round, ignoring him, cutting him off. 'I'm awfully sorry to have to tell you I didn't get to pass on your message.'

'Message?'

'About how much you'd always wanted him dead.'

'*Theos!* Saskia, I never should have said that. I lashed out at you. I didn't mean—'

'Of course you meant it! You meant every word. And all the time we were together, all the time you were making love to me, you still hated my father so much you wanted him dead. How you must have hated having anything to do with *me*, the daughter of the man you hated so deeply. Frankly, I'm surprised you could bear to touch me.'

'It wasn't like that.'

She held up a hand to silence him, her smile thin. 'Don't worry. It doesn't matter. What does matter is that you got your wish.'

Silence hung over the small kitchen like a shroud.

'What are you talking about?'

'Didn't you know? My father died yesterday.'

All of a sudden the dark circles around eyes almost too large in the unearthly pallor of her skin of her face made sense.

Victor Prentice was dead.

'Saskia,' he said, automatically reaching out for her, thinking back to when his own parents had died, remembering the awful sense of loss, knowing how terrible she must be feeling without him having unceremoniously dumped the news of Carmen's death on her as well.

Clumsily she darted out of his reach across the kitchen, putting the dining table between them and crossing her arms defensively in front of her. 'Don't you dare touch me!'

'Saskia…'

'And please don't insult my intelligence by pretending you're sorry! You wanted him dead all along. You must be so relieved he's finally out of the way.'

'No. I'm not going to pretend I ever liked or respected your father,' he said honestly, 'but I was wrong about him. And I was wrong to tell you what I did. I hurt you, and I shouldn't have.'

She blinked, her green eyes glossy and as hard as jade. 'What do you care about me anyway? I never meant more to you than a means of revenge—somebody you could thoroughly humiliate in order to satisfy your own personal need for vengeance.'

'That's not true,' he argued. 'The last thing I ever wanted was to humiliate you.'

Her eyes looked bigger than ever. Brilliant green pools of disbelief.

'And you don't think you did? I don't believe you. You led

me on, you took me out and made me feel like a princess—
and I did—I've never felt so special in my life. And once
you'd got me in the palm of your hand—*whammo*—you not
only pulled the rug out from under my feet, you did it when
I was at my most vulnerable, when I was naked in your bed.
Don't you have any concept of how humiliating that was?'

He bowed his head, knowing every word of what she said
was true. 'Believe me, I didn't want that.'

'Then what the hell did you think you were doing? Don't
you remember how you used me? Oh, my—' She stopped,
clamping one hand over her mouth. 'Why didn't I see it before?
All this time I thought you just wanted to humiliate my family
because of what my father had done in ruining your father's
business. But you had an even better reason. You took me to
bed because you were replaying what my father had done to
your sister. As if what he did wasn't bad enough, you had to
repeat the act! What kind of monster does that make you?'

'Listen, Saskia—' He moved in closer.

She moved back, every movement strained and wary,
screaming muscles on red alert.

'That was why you took me to bed, wasn't it? You were
performing the ultimate revenge. You took me to bed—purely
to get back at my father for what he'd done to Marla!'

He stood motionless. 'It's true. I was going to take your
virginity just as your father had taken Marla's. But I couldn't
do it. I couldn't go through with it. That's why I stopped.'

'You didn't stop! You threw me out of bed.'

'Because I didn't want to hurt you.'

'Don't give me that. You threw me out of bed because you're
a cold-hearted bastard. You don't care about anything or
anyone apart from your own sister, who doesn't even want your
help. And you're too arrogant and full of yourself to realise it.'

'No! Don't you see? If I'd been the cold-hearted bastard you accuse me of being, I wouldn't have thrown you out of bed. I would have stayed there, forced my way into you and finished the deed!'

'But you told me—'

Oh, yes, he remembered only too well what he'd told her that night. Hadn't she reminded him of it only recently? 'I didn't throw you out of bed because you were a virgin.'

She swallowed, her throat scratchy and dry. 'Then…why?'

'Because I couldn't do what I'd planned to. I'd worked it all out like a military operation. I had your father's business in striking distance and I had you exactly where I wanted. I had *everything* I wanted, all lined up like ducks in a row.'

'I trusted you!'

'I know. But you have to listen,' he implored. 'Because all the time I was with you—taking you out to dinner or the movies or dancing, supposedly getting you ripe for the picking so I could reap my revenge—I started to care for you. I wasn't expecting to. It was the last thing I wanted. But you were bright and fun and so beautiful, and it was no hardship to be with you. You were easy to like. But I had the memory of what your father had done to Marla and I had a goal—and I was determined that *nothing* was going to keep me from that.'

He paused, looking at her face, at the pain of the past merging with the pain of her recent loss, and he wished he could rewrite the past to make the present somehow more tolerable for her.

'I had it all planned,' he continued. 'I took you to the beach house. There'd be no interruptions—nobody would know we were there because I never took anyone there. And, just like I'd planned, you were ready for me. When I asked you to make love to me you came willingly. You let me take off your clothes and lie you down amongst the pillows.' He held up one hand, his index finger and thumb a bare millimetre apart. 'I was *this* close to taking what I wanted. I was *this* close to exacting my revenge.' He sighed.

'What happened? What changed your mind?'

'It was something you said that suddenly made me realise what kind of person I was becoming. All of a sudden I understood what I'd been doing ever since I was twelve years old and clawing my way up the ladder to get back everything my parents had lost and more. I'd never realised it for all those years, but you made me see just how far I'd sunk.'

'And that's why you dropped out of business society? It wasn't Marla?'

'No. It wasn't Marla. It was me, and the man I'd made myself into. And it was an ugly revelation. You made me realise that in seeking my revenge, in becoming a ruthless businessman and committing the same atrocious act your father had, I was turning into the very man I hated most in the world. I was so ashamed that from then on I knew I had to live a different life. I could still be successful, but I didn't need the ruthless tactics. I didn't need to be front-page news. I chose to hide away. Just like you guessed while we were in New York I had things I never wanted anyone to know, because it was hard enough facing them myself.'

He moved closer, and this time she didn't back away. He reached for her hands, cradling them in his own. 'Don't you understand? I knew I was going to hurt you, whatever I did that night, and I knew you would hate me. But I figured that at least I wouldn't rob you of everything. At least you'd still have something to offer someone else. Someone who might even deserve it—God knows, I didn't.'

She swallowed, the action pulling his attention to her lips and the long smooth ride of her throat. 'What was it I said?'

He smiled weakly, remembering the way she'd lain under him, her eyes so full of trust, her arms wrapped so tightly around his neck, her body so welcoming. 'You told me you loved me.'

Silence followed his words, allowing the sounds of the ticking mantel clock to fill the void, unnaturally loud in the ensuing silence.

'I thought I did back then,' she said softly at last, her voice barely more than a whisper, her use of the past tense slicing through his flesh like a scythe. 'I thought I was the luckiest woman on earth.'

He reached out, putting a hand to her hair, still damp and fresh from her shower, resting his forearm on her shoulder. Her scent, fresh and unadulterated, wove its way through him—the scent he'd missed so much since he'd walked out of their hotel suite days ago. He inhaled it, drinking her in, worried that this might well be the last time.

'Saskia, I'm so sorry.' Sorry for what he'd done. Sorry for what her words revealed. She *had* loved him—in the past. Was there no chance of rekindling that love? Was there no hope at all for their future now?

'You were so angry with me that night. I don't think I've ever been more afraid.'

He toyed with the loose spiral ends of her hair, running them through his fingers. 'I know. You bore the brunt of it, but I was furious with *me*—disgusted for letting myself sink to such depths. I'd been so completely blindsided by my desperate need for revenge that I couldn't see what was in front of me—that I cared for you and that it meant something that you loved me. But I knew that I'd just ruined whatever chance I might have had with you. I knew I had to find a reason to throw you out of my bed and that it had to be one that would make you hate me for what I had done. Can you ever forgive me?'

'It's okay,' she said, closing her eyes to his ministrations as two fat tears rolled down her cheeks. 'Under the circumstances, I guess I should thank you for sparing me the same fate as your sister.'

Her words speared into his conscience. He touched the other hand to her cheek, brushing the tears away, feeling her tremble and feeling his own guilt build up by another layer. 'It's not okay. Because I never should have had you in my bed. Not for the reasons I used. I got it all wrong. Your father never raped my sister.'

Her eyes widened and she leaned back away from him. His hand was still on her shoulder. She anchored a hand on his forearm as if to steady herself.

'What did you say?'

'I spoke to Marla. It wasn't how I thought.'

'What do you mean? Are you saying they didn't have sex?'

He took a moment to steady her. 'They did, and she *was* only fifteen, but Marla insists it was hardly forced. In fact she maintains that he was reluctant but she pursued him—that she all but threw herself at him.'

Saskia sniffed, and touched the back of her hand to her nose.

'But what about him flaunting the fact he'd taken her virginity in front of your parents like you told me? Was that not true either?'

Alex sighed. 'That much he *did* do. He told my father he'd taken Marla's virginity as part of the deal.'

'But why would he do that?'

Alex ground his teeth together. 'Apparently he wasn't proud of what he'd done, but there was no way he wanted the truth to come out. He let my parents think he'd stolen her virginity so that they would hate him and not turn against her. In his own way, it seems he was protecting her.'

She blinked her haunted eyes, and he could see how much effort she was putting into holding herself together, but there were at least the beginnings of something like hope in her features.

'So you're saying my father was never a rapist?'

'No,' he said quietly. 'And I wish I could take back all those ugly words I hurled at you. I wish I could have saved you that. I was so wrong.'

'You thought you were avenging your sister. I can't imagine anyone going to such lengths for *me*.'

I would, he thought. If only I had a chance.

Saskia took a deep breath and moved across the kitchen, wiping her face with her hands. 'I should thank you for coming and explaining everything. Especially for what you just told me. I appreciate you coming so far to clear it up.'

He froze. She was dismissing him. And he hadn't finished what he'd come here to tell her. But she was still raw from her father's death, and she'd had enough to assimilate for one day.

'Then I'll go,' he said.

Saskia tied her ponytail with a black satin ribbon and stood back to survey her reflection, tugging on the hem of her black jacket. The dark circles were still there under her eyes. Make-up had made them less obvious, and lipstick had given her face some much needed colour, but overall… She grimaced. How was she expected to sleep anyway? She would have to do as she was. It was hardly a fashion parade after all.

She glanced at her watch and took a deep breath. It was time. In a strange way she was looking forward to the funeral. These last two days she'd done a lot of thinking about her father—missing him dreadfully, contemplating life without him, but thankful also that he had been spared possibly months in a coma. At least the end, when it had come, had come blessedly quickly.

And the funeral would be some kind of closure. She knew now how it must have been with Marla and her father—a pretty young girl, a lonely man missing his wife. It hadn't been the right thing, but thank heavens it wasn't as bad as she'd first feared. At least now she knew.

She gathered up her handbag and keys and pulled open the door to meet the gloomy grey day, heading out to meet the cab that would be here any minute.

'Can I offer you a lift?'

She took a step back. The dark-suited figure leaning against the sleek black Jaguar was the last thing she'd been expecting to see outside her door.

'What are you doing here? I thought you'd gone.'

He *had* gone. She'd sent him away herself, and he had left as smoothly as the chiffon dress she'd sent to charity had slipped through her fingers. He'd done what he'd come for. He'd made his apologies and given her plenty to think about.

Surely he should already be back ruling his empire from Sydney, or Tahoe, or wherever it was that he was based right now? Why was he still hanging around here?

'I came to take you to the funeral.'

'I don't think so,' she said, knowing she wasn't strong enough today to deal with both the loss of her father and Alex's presence. 'You spent your entire life hating my father. Do you think there's a chance in hell I'd let you take me to his funeral?'

He straightened and looked her in the eyes, his charcoal gaze steady and direct.

'I told you why I felt that way. And I told you I was wrong.'

'Yes,' she agreed. 'You were wrong.'

'But my being here today has nothing to do with how I felt about your father. This has everything to do with how I feel about you.'

She was too tired to work out what he meant. Instead she looked up and down the street. 'I've ordered a cab.'

'And I've sent it away.'

'You did what?' She shook her head and dived into her purse for her keys. 'Then maybe I'll take my car after all.'

'You shouldn't drive—not today. Do you have someone else to take you?'

Her sideways look told him everything he needed to know. There was no one else. She was alone. And she'd had no intention of driving.

'Then I'll take you,' he decided.

'You might have asked if you could come.'

'And you would have let me?'

'No.'

Ten minutes later he pulled into a parking space outside the small funeral chapel and killed the engine. She made no move to get out of the car.

'You'll feel better once it's over.'

She looked at him, her eyes so filled with grief and despair he just wanted to take her in his arms and hold her. But instead he took her hand and squeezed it gently. 'Come on,' he said.

There were few in attendance. Enid Sharpe from next door, his visiting nurse and a couple of old cronies he'd played bridge with. Throughout the brief ceremony she held herself together, the strain etched in lines around her eyes and mouth as she contemplated the flower strewn coffin bearing her father.

Bearing the man Alex had hated for almost a quarter of a century. And all for what? A pointless exercise in revenge for something that had never happened. And now what did he have to show for all that hate? What had it produced but more problems? Marla had been so right. It was time to let it go.

At the end of the service he felt Saskia's hand slip into his, and he looked down into the green pools of her eyes. 'Thank you for bringing me,' she said, before Enid came up to give her a hug.

Afterwards they stayed only long enough for a cup of tea, exchanging small talk with the minister.

She slumped back in her seat when he got her into the car, her head tipped back, her eyes closed. 'Thank God that's over,' she said on a sigh.

She looked exhausted, and from the way her black suit bagged around her he suspected it was days since she'd eaten properly. She was just about asleep before they made it back to her flat. He carried her in, despite her protests.

'Would you like me to run you a bath?' he asked.

She shook her head. 'No, just bed,' she muttered sleepily, her arms around his neck, her face nestled into his chest.

He carried her to her room and pulled back the covers, placing her gently down. He slid off her shoes and peeled away the baggy suit without protest from her, shocked at how much flesh had wasted from her bones. She shivered, and he tucked the blankets closer around her.

'So cold,' she whispered, trembling.

He couldn't leave her like that. He pulled off his own shoes and stripped off his suit in a moment, joining her in the bed, collecting her into his arms and wrapping himself around her. She clung to him and cuddled closer, her head resting on his shoulder, her legs scissored between his, and he willed his heat into her, feeling her trembling gradually subside and her breathing steady as she drifted towards sleep.

He kissed her hair, breathed in the sweet scent of her and tucked her closer.

'I love you,' he said. *'Agape mou.'*

CHAPTER TWELVE

SASKIA woke up feeling better than she had for days. She must have slept for hours, filled with dreams of warmth and loving. And then she remembered. *Alex.* She spun around, but she was alone and her heart pitched south. He'd been so good to her yesterday, so gentle and understanding. Surely he couldn't have left? But why had he been here in the first place? He'd made his apologies. What could he still want with her now?

Her bedroom door swung open. 'Perfect timing.' Alex smiled at her as he came around the door, still wearing the dark suit trousers and white shirt of yesterday, but with the sleeves rolled up and the buttons left undone, exposing a tantalising glimpse of firm olive-skinned torso. But right now it was the tray he was carrying that snagged her attention, piled high with plates and cups and from which the most heavenly smells were coming. 'Are you hungry?'

She took another long look at that patch of skin, and the whirl of hairs that disappeared down into his trousers. He looked good enough to eat himself, but her stomach was sounding a definite protest. 'Famished,' she said, surprised at how true it was. She hadn't felt like eating for days, and suddenly her body seemed to want to make up for it.

'You go wash up,' he said. 'I'll get the coffee.'

She skipped out of bed, grabbing her robe and making for the bathroom, horrified at her reflection. Hair everywhere, and yesterday's make-up sliding wherever, but at least her eyes didn't look so hollow any more. She rinsed her face and attacked her curls with a comb.

'Back into bed,' he ordered when she reappeared, and she didn't think to argue, too busy contemplating the plates piled with eggs, bacon and tomatoes, the racks of toast and dishes of butter and jam.

He loaded up a plate and handed it to her, and it was all she could do not to inhale it all in one delicious whoosh.

'Oh, my,' she said, sipping on a coffee as she leaned back against her headboard. 'That was wonderful.'

'You've had enough?'

'Hold the dessert,' she joked as she patted her tummy. 'Seriously, thank you,' she said. 'Not just for breakfast, but for everything you did for me yesterday. I was so tired last night, so cold, and you kept me warm and safe. And I didn't think I wanted you at the funeral but I'm glad you were there.'

He topped up her coffee and set the plates aside. 'It was important for me too. I carried around that hatred for so long—too long—it was time to let it go. I'd been so wrong about everything, so damned stupid, but all along he was your father, and he'd made a beautiful daughter in you. How could I hate him?'

She smiled, tears springing into her eyes. 'Oh, hell,' she said, reaching for a box of tissues. 'I thought I was done with the tears.'

He laughed softly, moving closer, taking the tissue and touching it gently to her eyes, soaking up the moisture. She blinked her eyes open, studying his eyes, so close to her own.

'Why are you still here?'

He leaned back, his charcoal eyes so desperately focused on hers she could feel the communication between them. 'There's something I have to ask you. I want to know if you can ever forgive me for what I did and for all the hurt I've caused you.'

'You've apologised already.'

'No,' he said. 'That wasn't enough. I need to know if you forgive me, because only then can we really put what's happened behind us.'

She hesitated. 'And that's important because…?'

'Because then we have a chance at a future together. If you want one. Because I love you, Saskia. God knows I don't deserve you, but I don't want to spend my future apart from you.'

'You love me?' She blinked, remembering those words from a dream, warm and loving and happy. But this was far better than the foggy memory of a distant dream. Far better. This was real.

He smiled. 'I love you. It took me a long time to realise it—much too long. But I want to spend my life loving you, if you'll have me.'

'You love me,' she said again, in awe and wonder, her lips curling at the sound of the words, at their taste on her tongue, at the way they fed her soul.

He laughed, a rich, deep sound that radiated warmth. 'Can I take it you don't mind, then?'

'Don't mind? Do you know how long I've waited to hear those words from you?'

'And do you know how much I've missed hearing those words from you? You said it to me once. But I'll understand if you can never bring yourself to say it to me again.'

'Oh, Alex.' She shook her head. 'I tried not to,' she said. 'I really tried to stop loving you. For so long I told myself I hated you, that I couldn't possibly love you. But, damn you, I've always loved you, Alex Koutoufides. I never stopped loving you, and I never stopped hoping one day that I'd hear you say those words to me. Of course I love you.'

'Saskia,' he said, pulling her into his arms. 'You don't know how good it is to hear that from you. Because I love you so very much. And I have so much to make up for.'

And he kissed her, a kiss so achingly sweet and full of love it moved her soul. This was the man she was destined to be with. This was her mate. This was her destiny. All those years ago, as a seventeen-year-old young woman, she'd known it. And all these years later it was finally coming to pass.

His kiss told her how much he loved her and how much he wanted her. His hands moved over her, his touch like worship, cherishing her, seducing her, setting her body alight while her hands pushed their way under his shirt, desperate to get closer, itching to feel more of the muscled wall of his chest.

'About that dessert…' he whispered, his breathing already choppy as he ripped off his shirt and tugged at the ties of her robe.

'Bring it on.' She chuckled as she dragged him back down to her lips. 'Didn't I tell you I was famished?'

EPILOGUE

BLISS. Life could never get better than this.

Saskia paused as she looked out onto the enclosed patio of their Tahoe home, watching Alex cradle the tiny bundle that was his month-old daughter on his jeans-covered legs.

Their daughter.

The daughter they'd made together in an act of love.

He looked down at baby Sophie so adoringly that she sucked in a lungful of pure happiness. She loved him so much. Even now she got a thrill thinking of her name aligned with his. Even after a year of marriage the wonder was still there.

And tiny Sophie's arrival had magnified that wonder tenfold.

She picked up two of the salads the housekeeper had prepared earlier and stepped out onto the deck, placing them on the table, watching his face light up with warmth as he welcomed her approach.

'What time are our visitors arriving?'

'Any minute now. I hope you've got the champagne chilling. Marla told me they've got an announcement to make.'

He looked up quickly, still with Sophie's tiny hands clinging to his fingers, as Saskia sat down in the chair alongside. 'Are you thinking what I'm thinking?'

She nodded. 'Oh, yes. Jake's the one. They've been

together a good while now, and he's good for her. He's solid and loyal, and she'll need that stability—especially now she's going to be doing this book tour. It's obvious they've been crazy about each other for ages, despite all her protests to the contrary. I'm glad they're planning on making it official.'

'She's so different now,' he said, gazing back into his baby's big dark eyes. 'So much more self-assured. The book's success has been amazing.'

'I think Marla's found herself. She has her own career now, with her writing. You know she's picked up another national monthly column? She actually feels like she's making her own way in the world, and she's loving it.'

'And you're responsible for that.'

She shook her head. 'No, Marla is. She's the one who took control of her life. All we had to do was help her make it happen. And you letting go the reins had as much to do with it as I did.'

He looked at her with equal measures of respect and love. 'You will never stop astounding me, you know. I think I might just love you, Mrs Koutoufides.'

'I think I might just love you back, Mr Koutoufides.'

He snaked an arm around her neck and pulled her in, kissing her over the squirming baby below. 'So, what's next for your own career? Have you given Marla's offer any more thought?'

She nodded. 'I'm going to tell her today. I'll take on her press work—it should be fun—and I'll fit in my own freelance articles when I get a chance. It should be the perfect stay-at-home job.'

'You don't miss *AlphaBiz*?' he asked, when finally he let her go.

She smiled, and touched a finger to the baby-soft curls adorning Sophie's head. 'What kind of a question is that? No. I wasn't happy with the way they seemed to be going anyway—increasingly chasing the celebrity angle. I don't want to write that way. Besides,' she said, smiling into the dark eyes of her young child, 'why would I rather be seeking out crusty old businessmen to interview when I can have the best of both worlds—doing freelance work and looking after this little one and her father?'

He scowled. 'Crusty old businessmen, eh?'

'Present company excluded,' she added with a grin. 'Anyone as gorgeously talented and virile as you can't be too crusty.'

He pulled her close again, measuring the ripe sway of her breasts in his free hand. 'Maybe later on I might be able to convince you just how virile and uncrusty I am.'

'I warn you now,' she said, already feeling her body awaken and stir at his sensual caress, 'I might take some convincing.'

He growled and pulled her close, and they shared a kiss so deep and rich with promise that it was only the plaintive cry of the child on his lap that broke it off. He turned his attentions back to his child, scooping her up into his arms, kissing her softly on the forehead.

'Was I neglecting you, sweetheart?'

Her cries stilled, her eyes locking onto her father's, her tiny mouth stretching into a wide, gummy smile.

'She smiled at me!' He looked at Saskia. 'Look at that! They said she wouldn't do that until at she was at least six weeks old.'

'Of course she smiled at you,' she responded, stroking the downy dark hair of little Sophie. 'How could she resist? I never could.'

He beamed back at her. 'And, when it comes to the women in my life, that's just the way I like it.'

He contemplated the child in his arms again, and breathed in deep as he looked back at the woman he loved. 'I love you,

Saskia, for your warmth and your beauty and for giving me this child. But most of all for your forgiveness and your love. You've made me the happiest man in the entire world.'

She wrapped her arms around both the man she loved and the tiny baby cradled in his arms, feeling the love radiating out from him and breathing in the magic scent of pure one hundred per cent male mixed with the sweet, innocent smell of a newborn.

It was a mix that moved her like no other.

It was love she could sense.

It was intoxicating.

It was simply…

Bliss.

HARLEQUIN *Presents*

Passion and Seduction Guaranteed!

She's sexy, successful and pregnant!

Relax and enjoy our fabulous series about couples whose passion results in pregnancies… sometimes unexpected!

Share the surprises, emotions, drama and suspense as our parents-to-be come to terms with the prospect of bringing a new life into the world. All will discover that the business of making babies brings with it the most special joy of all….

February's Arrival:

PREGNANT BY THE MILLIONAIRE

by Carole Mortimer

What happens when Hebe Johnson finds out she's pregnant with her noncommittal boss's baby?

Find out when you buy your copy of this title today!

REQUEST YOUR FREE BOOKS!

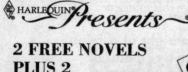

HARLEQUIN *Presents*

PASSION
GUARANTEED
SEDUCTION

2 FREE NOVELS PLUS 2 FREE GIFTS!

YES! Please send me 2 FREE Harlequin Presents® novels and my 2 FREE gifts. After receiving them, if I don't wish to receive any more books, I can return the shipping statement marked "cancel." If I don't cancel, I will receive 6 brand-new novels every month and be billed just $3.80 per book in the U.S., or $4.47 per book in Canada, plus 25¢ shipping and handling per book and applicable taxes, if any*. That's a savings of close to 15% off the cover price! I understand that accepting the 2 free books and gifts places me under no obligation to buy anything. I can always return a shipment and cancel at any time. Even if I never buy another book from Harlequin, the two free books and gifts are mine to keep forever.

106 HDN EEXK 306 HDN EEXV

Name	(PLEASE PRINT)	
Address		Apt. #
City	State/Prov.	Zip/Postal Code

Signature (if under 18, a parent or guardian must sign)

Mail to the Harlequin Reader Service®:

IN U.S.A.	**IN CANADA**
P.O. Box 1867	P.O. Box 609
Buffalo, NY	Fort Erie, Ontario
14240-1867	L2A 5X3

Not valid to current Harlequin Presents subscribers.

Want to try two free books from another line?
Call 1-800-873-8635 or visit www.morefreebooks.com.

* Terms and prices subject to change without notice. NY residents add applicable sales tax. Canadian residents will be charged applicable provincial taxes and GST. This offer is limited to one order per household. All orders subject to approval. Credit or debit balances in a customer's account(s) may be offset by any other outstanding balance owed by or to the customer. Please allow 4 to 6 weeks for delivery.